Taste the Flavors

Stella Regina Maris

Taste the Flavors

Last winter and on into early spring, she spent some time — hours, in fact — sitting in an old coffee house, downtown. You know the one — it has a wooden floor that creaks when you step on just the right floorboards and heavy glass windows, from floor to ceiling. After a while, she began to notice that a group of half a dozen women came in every week — sometimes in pairs, sometimes three or four at a time, and several times, all six together. They would sit in a secluded corner table at the back of the shop, next to one of the windows. She didn't remember if it was the reflection of headlights on the window by their table or the fragments of their conversation she overheard that first caught her attention . . .

1.

A banger for breakfast

. . .

Sara's story

"I was just thinking how much I love sucking you," I said. "I want to suck your cock."

"Suck me," he said, "suck me . . ."

I once fell head over heels for a man from across the seas, whom I met at midnight while traveling. He was intent on talking to me throughout the flight, never mind how badly I wanted to sleep. At some point during the hours we spent talking, he slipped my left hand into his large, warm right hand and whenever he gestured with his hands, my hand moved in the air with his, so for the rest of the conversation, it was though each of us had somehow become one being -- moving, speaking, and thinking in unison.

When I could not stay awake and listen to him any longer, no matter how much I wanted to, he wrapped his arms around me and pulled me close to his chest and held me until I woke up when the plane was landing in the early dawn. He held me like that every time afterwards too, every time we were together, after we made love and fell asleep, he always put his arms around me and pulled me next to his chest and held me close to him until we woke up.

From the moment he first met me, he looked at me as though he adored me, as though I were some magical creature who had dropped down from the heavens. His voice was so tender whenever he spoke to me, I felt like I had walked into a dream. Most of the time, we were separated by miles and miles of land and sea, but it was as though we were together every day, because he called me every morning to say good morning and every evening to say goodnight with hot passionate sexy words that left me dreaming of being with him throughout the night. Lots of times too, we made hot hot love to each other over the phone and across the internet by text and email, off and on throughout the day and into the night. I found I was walking on air every hour of every day and the stars he put in my eyes could have lit up the night.

The morning of the first weekend we spent together, I cooked him breakfast, a big British fry-up. I asked him how he wanted his eggs. "One egg, cooked," he said, leaving me to wonder if that meant fried, scrambled, boiled, or poached, "and one rasher of bacon -- you can see how fat I've gotten by traveling so much and eating all this American food." He looked so serious when he spoke, then suddenly he smiled, which made his eyes twinkle as he patted his stomach.

"I have gotten some bangers for breakfast, too," I said, using the British term for the large pink sausages sold in every butcher shop throughout the United Kingdom. "What," he said, "do you mean link sausages?" "No, proper British bangers, I found them at the butcher's in the organic food market," I said and he laughed. So bangers it was for breakfast that day.

Even later on, after he stumbled and lost hold of me, so that I crashed to earth amid the shards of the fallen stars and I was left reeling as though I'd been punched straight through my heart -- all the way through my heart -- I was surprised to find I still liked him and my body wanted him beyond anything or anyone else, so from time to time -- not as often as before, but just as passionately -- we still met. I would always suck his cock as soon as we pulled our clothes off and I would suck him again before we parted, after we had fucked each other until we couldn't fuck anymore and I was too sore to walk without remembering how every inch of his cock felt inside me. "Give me your come," I'd say, taking my mouth off his large, hard, pink cock long enough to say a few words between sucking him, "give it to me, I want it more than you do, it's mine, your come is mine, just give it to me, stop trying to keep it to yourself, I want it, I want you to come in my mouth."

During those times when we had the whole night with each other, I would wake him up the next morning by running my tongue up and down his cock, which would be hard and ready for me, even though he was still asleep. I would wrap my lips around it, then I would take it deep into my mouth and sometimes even deeper into my throat. I would run my lips and my tongue over it until he woke up and started stroking inside my mouth, slowly at first, then harder and faster, stroking and stroking inside my mouth, until he couldn't hold back anymore and his come exploded all down my throat, inside my mouth, and over my tongue, salty and wet like the sea.

To this day, I can still see his large pink cock, hard and standing straight up, rising up from its lovely thick nest of coppery-gold pubic hair while he sleeps and I think how much I love to suck him awake in the morning, suck his cock until he explodes in my mouth and I swallow his come, then lick his cock shiny clean before breakfast. I want so much to suck him, now, right now, just like I do in the morning, every morning of every day we are together -- suck him until his hot, salty come

that tastes like the sea floods out of him and
fills up my mouth.

2.

The foot massage

. . .

Marilyn's story

He said, "I want to give you a foot massage."

I'm thinking, OK, but you ain't going to get nothing, honey.

This guy I know, six foot nine, came into the bar where we went after we finished all the rehearsals. He looked at me and came up, hugged me and gave me a kiss on the cheek. He said, you looked beautiful -- I heard about the rehearsal on your website, so I came to watch you.

We danced in the club until I told him I'm really tired, I have to go home -- I'm going to turn into a pumpkin at midnight. He said, I'm following you. I'm thinking, OK, but you ain't going to get nothing, honey.

He said, I want to give you a foot massage. He followed me in his car back to the apartment, then he came in and sat on the couch in the living room. He said, go take a shower. I said this will take me a while. He said, I have time, so I took a nice long shower and I cleaned my feet so they would be nice and soft.

I put my bathrobe on and I came to the living room and asked him if he needed something to drink. He said, water, so I got him water and made tea for me, then I sat right next to him on the couch. He asked me where were the music channels on my TV. I asked him what type of music do you want to listen to. He said some soul, R&B, and slow jam.

Then he asked me for my massage oil and took my feet and massaged them for about 20 minutes. I thought, oh my god you can do whatever you want to do to me, honey. After he finished, I was like oh-h-h, that felt so good because my feet were hurting from wearing the heels all day. Then he laid his head closer on my shoulder and I started massaging his head. He said, I love this, and I said I can do this all night. Then he touched my chest and played with my nipples and I was like, oh-h-h.

He started kissing me on my chest, then he got up and laid my legs on the couch. He dropped on his knees and started kissing me all over and opened my bathrobe. He took my bathrobe belt -- the two ends of the belt are very soft -- and caressed my body with it. He saw my tattoo, which is a saxophone right above my coochie. He looked at me and he said I like that, you make your own beat, how about you start playing a song?

He went down on me and started playing and, mind you, he was on his knees next to my couch so he could access me better. He didn't touch my coochie with his hand, only with his tongue. He had really soft lips and he licked it very softly and gently until he found my clit. Then he turned off the music because he said, I want to listen to your song -- he meant my moaning. Then he stopped and I was like -- ah what the heck? He said I don't have a condom. I said you don't need a condom, just finish my song. He said, I was planning on doing that anyway. He went back down and finished and I came. It was so nice -- I liked how sensual he was. He kissed me and he tasted so good, with my juices all over his mouth. He said he had been looking forward to doing this for a long time.

He started laughing and he zipped himself up. I said, what, are you going to go home and take care of that, meaning his hard, stiff dick and he said well . . . He dropped his pants and sat down right next to me. I touched my coochie -- it was really wet. I took my juices and put them on top of his penis and used my juices to jerk him off. I started kissing his ear and his cheek and his neck and I was stroking his penis. While I was doing that, he grabbed my hair and it got all tangled up. He was pulling my hair harder and harder -- I knew he

was getting ready to come. I said ohhh,
someone is getting ready to spit it out.

The only thing I didn't like was that he
was uncircumcised and I haven't touched an
uncircumcised dick in a long time. The whole
time I was stroking his big black dick, I was
thinking what a waste that I can't jump on it
yet, but it is not the time yet -- still, looking at
his dick turned me on even more. I kept
stroking him until he came.   There was a lot of
come -- it was all over and came all through
my fingers, so I told him to stay right there and
not move. I brought him a warm washcloth
and I cleaned him up -- he was leaning back,
just chilling, with his eyes closed -- I knew he
enjoyed it.

After I cleaned him up, I gave him a little
kiss on his tip of his penis and put his pants
back on and said, thank you, meaning it is
time for you to go.

3.

I give good baths

. . .

Stella's story

"I'm heading to bed with a photo of you that shows off your tits ... turn me on, make me come while I look at you . . ."

Subject: **Midday**

Scott,

Going to lunch ...
I have been thinking about that picture of your cock I
asked for (the picture I haven't seen because you haven't
sent it to me) all morning ...

Xxx Stella x

Subject: **RE: Midday**

LOL I was very horny last night -- I deleted it
from my phone when it wouldn't send xx Scott

Subject: **Re: Midday**

Just so I get a picture sometime, maybe sooner than later
(of course, greeting your cock in person again, face to
mouth will be best of all). . .

Still very horny for you, mmmmm sexy man

Xxx Stella x

Subject: RE: Midday

Looking forward to it also xxxx Scott

~Later on, in the evening

Subject: hi

Hello xx
I sent you something xx Scott

Subject: Re: hi

Just off work and back home. Walking in the door
About to open surprise from you

Xxx Stella x

Subject: Re: hi

Starting laptop. Can't wait. . .

Xxx Stella X

Subject: RE: hi

No dick LOL xx Scott

Subject: Re: hi

Yes, noticed that, but very nice new pictures of you. Now I have three, instead of just one. Love the pictures,

Xxx Stella x

Subject: RE: hi

xxx Scott

Subject: Re: hi

Putting them into photo album . . . The smiley one was taken in your office?

Xxx Stella x

Subject: RE: hi

yes xxx

Subject: Re: hi

Thank you (kisses) for the photos. Two from last year, before we met and one from this year. I love the photos.

Xxx Stella x

Subject: Re: hi

Scott,

Still looking at your pictures x   Lovely surprise x

xxx Stella x

Subject: Re: hi

I love your lips. I want to kiss them.

xxx Stella x (going to take off work clothes, back in a mo)

~An hour later on

Subject: RE: hi

Where are you xxx Scott

Subject: Re: hi

I fell asleep holding laptop xxx

I'm awake now, a little groggy . . .

xxx Stella x

Subject: xxx

Where are you, Scott?

xxx Stella x

Subject: RE: xxx

I am here -- turn me on xx Scott

Subject: Re: xxx

What are you wearing? I have on dark red lipstick and a smile. . .

Xxx Stella x

Subject: RE: xxx

Heading to bed with a hope that u will make me come as I look at u xxx Scott

Subject: **Re: xxx**

Which pic are you looking at?

Stella
xxx

Subject: **RE: xxx**

The smiley one of you from New Year xx Scott

Subject: **Re: xxx**

Scott,

I am standing beside your bed. I am naked . . .

Xxx Stella x

Subject: **RE: xxx**

Will I play with you x

Subject: Re: xxx

Yes . . . put your hand in my cunt . . .

tell me to open my legs

Xxx Stella x

Subject: RE: xxx

Open your legs xx tell me what you want x Scott

Subject: Fwd: xxx

Put your thumb on my clit. Massage it as you move your fingers inside me . . .

xxx Stella x

Subject: RE: xxx

That would be wonderful -- my thumb is in you xx Scott

Subject: Re: xxx

I want your mouth on my cunt

I want your tongue on my pussy lips

I want your tongue licking my clit

xxx Stella x

Subject: **RE: xxx**

I am now licking you xx Scott

Subject: **Re: xxx**

Put your hands on my buttocks

xxx Stella x

Subject: **RE: xxx**

My hands are on your buttocks and I am licking you x Scott

Subject: **Fwd: xxx**

Pull me to you and bury your face in my pussy

I am not going to be able to stand up much longer . . .

xxx Stella

Subject: RE: xxx

Keep standing xx

I'm not letting you move away x Scott

Subject: Re: xxx

I am moving back and forth toward your mouth and away from your mouth . . . my cunt is very hot . . .

What do you want me to do to you, I ask, I love this what you are doing to me I love your mouth on my cunt

Molten for you . . .

X Stella xxx

Subject: Re: xxx

I push you back on the bed and am over you, you are still licking me. . .

X Stella xxx

Subject: RE: xxx

I love sucking you - no need yet to do anything to me x Scott

Subject: RE: xxx

My finger and tongue are in you xx Scott

Subject: Fwd: xxx

I am on top of your face, I turn around to face your cock while you are still licking me, I want to lick your balls. I want my mouth on your dick. . .

Stella xxx

Subject: Re: xxx

You don't let me get to you, Scott, you hold me back and you keep licking me. I am going wild. I want my mouth on you. . . Let me suck you.

Xxx Stella x

Subject: RE: xxx

I want you to suck me xx Scott

Subject: Re: xxx

Oh yes, Scott,

I run my tongue up your dick and round the top. I kiss your belly and then run my mouth down to the base of your cock . .

Mmm xxx Stella

Subject: RE: xxx

Suck my balls and everything else you see xxx Scott

Subject: Re: xxx

I am licking around the base of your penis. I am going around the side. Now I am at your balls. I am licking them. I open my mouth. . . and they are in my mouth. . .

X Stella x

Subject: RE: xxx

Do you love licking my balls xx? Scott

Subject: Re: xxx

Yes - yes - yes, Scott, I love your balls . . . I love the curly golden hair they lie in.

I love tracing their round shapes with my tongue. . .

I curl my tongue around them again and again and pull my lips tight against you, just below your balls xxx

Stella xx

Subject: RE: xxx

Tell me more xxx lick me where you want x Scott

Subject: Fwd: xxx

My tongue is rolling around your balls my lips suck your balls. I move them out and move down a bit.

My mouth is kissing you between your balls and your anus. My tongue is licking you.

Xxx Stella x

Subject: RE: xxx

I am heading to bed give me a mo xx Scott

Subject: Re: xxx

Not without me, I am going with you . . .

Stella xxx

Subject: Fwd: xxx

Scott, I am on fire for you. . .

X Stella

Subject: Fwd: xxx

Scott, I can't keep my hands off you . . .

X Stella

Subject: RE: xxx

Stella, I am lying buck naked in bed now — what a turn on xx you kissing me and licking behind my balls xx Scott

Subject: **Re: xxx**

I can give good baths and massages too, as well as licking you like nothing else . . . and I can do lots of other things too . . .

Xxx Stella x

Subject: **RE: xxx**

Oh baths, I love a good bath. Tell me more xxx Scott

Subject: **Re: xxx**

You want a bath in a bathtub or maybe one in bed xxx?

X Stella

Subject: **RE: xxx**

Both! LOL xxx Scott

Subject: **Re: xxx**

We can do that, Scott . . . nice hot soapy cloth

I start with your toes,
And rub all around them. . .

Then trace up your instep
And up your legs . . .

And now I'm at your crotch,
Oooo nice, I'm distracted. ..

X xx x xx x mmmmmm. . .

Subject: **RE: xxx**

Keep going xxx Scott

Subject: **Fwd: xxx**

I run the hot cloth all around your crotch mmmmm xxx

And up your crack
And over your butt . . .

And up your back

Now roll over on your belly . . . I need to feel more of you with my soapy cloth. . .

X Stella xxx

Subject: FW: xxx

Sent u a pic xx Scott

Subject: Re: xxx

Wow! wow! wow! Your lovely hard cock! Oh oh oh. At last. . . You sent me a picture of your cock! I'm really distracted now . . .

Xxx x Stella

Subject: RE: xxx

Tell me more xx, Stella

What would you do to me if you were here xx Scott

Subject: Fwd: xxx

Oh Scott, that picture of your cock looks so good, standing up, waiting for me to lick it . . . oh, oh, oh, I want your cock in my mouth, in my cunt . . .

Back to licking you (can't think straight. . . I love your cock . . .)

My mouth is at your toes and your feet and my tongue is licking you, straight up the insides of your legs to your cock Xxx Stella x

Subject: **RE: xxx**

I want you to turn me on xxx Scott

Subject: **Fwd: xxx**

Oh, Scott, I love your dick, put it in my mouth. I want your lovely great hard dick in my mouth. Xxx

X Stella xxx

Subject: **RE: xxx**

Yum — keep going xxx Scott

Subject: **Re: xxx**

I love your sucking my nipples. I am having a hard time typing. Your dick picture ah ah ah xxx xxx

Suck my nipples, Scott, bite my nipples. . .

X Stella xxx

Subject: **RE: xxx**

I love your nipples x Scott

Subject: **Re: xxx**

I'm moving up your chest to your arms . . .

And I drag the hot wet cloth onto your armpits and up your arms, then down to your fingers and back again Now I'm up to your neck and next . . .

I will rinse off the soap with warm water and then I lick you all over . . .

X Stella xxx

Subject: **RE: xxx**

Turn me on xxxx Scott

Subject: RE: xxx

My tongue has started back on your toes . . .I'm nibbling your instep
I want you, I want my face in your crotch, I want your dick in my mouth . . .

I will lick you up your thighs
Until I reach your crotch and your lovely hard dick
I will lick you and swirl my tongue around your hard pole
xxx

X Stella xxx

Subject: RE: xxx

Yummy - I am now stoking my hard cock xx Scott

Subject: RE: xxx

Scott,

I've decided my tits want to get in on this fun . . .

X Stella xxx

Subject: RE: xxx

Oh yes please xx Scott

Subject: Re: xxx

Scott,

I am dangling my breasts over your balls . . .
My nipples are tight and hard . . .

X Stella xxx

Subject: Re: xxx

I want your dick to side between my breasts
I want my tongue licking your dick as it strokes between
my breasts . . .

X Stella xxx

Subject: Re: xxx

I pinch your nipples xx I am very hard xx Scott

Subject: Re: xxx

*Oh my, oh my, I am so hot I am about to come, but I will
try not to come,
not just yet xx*

Oh, bite my nipples xxx Stella

Subject: Re: xxx

**r u coming xx
Where r your hands xx Scott**

Subject: Re: xxx

*One hand is at my breasts, Scott, going back and
forth between my nipples and twisting them so that they
are harder . . .*

Subject: Re: xxx

*The other hand is on my clit, rubbing it, pressing it
hard . . .*

X Stella xxx

Subject: Re: xxx

Every time you have your thumb and fingers on your clit, Stella, you know that's really my mouth on your clit, when you're rubbing your clit, it is really my mouth on it, it's my tongue that you are feeling. Always remember that -- it's my tongue xx Scott

Subject: Fwd: xxx

Mmmmm... My bottom is moving rolling back and forth toward and away from you . . .my pussy is hot for your dick inside and can't wait any longer

X Stella xxx

Subject: Fwd: xxx

Shall I call? Send me your number again xx xx Scott

Subject: RE: xxx

YES! Scott! Call! Very very hot . . . Want you so much

Here is my number . . .

Xxx Stella x

~ Ring-g-g . . .

4.

The man with the black card

. . .

Mariah's story

I guess the black card will buy you anything. . .

He was all over me, hugging me, kissing me, and telling me he missed me so much and I though, oh well, I'm hungry, I'm going to order a lot to eat. The hotel he stays in is beautiful, so I really enjoyed it. Do you know that he does Botox in his forehead? I didn't think he would do that, but I guess the black card will buy you anything. He gave me it to hold and I was like -- ooooh -- I didn't want to give it back.

As soon as I stepped up to his table and gave him a kiss, it was like a jolt of electricity went through him -- he started talking really loudly, telling his story, and introducing me to all the people at the table, and telling me it's so good to see you.

He had already ordered a bottle of my favorite wine, riesling, since he knew what I liked. When he asked me about my business and said he liked my website, his phone started ringing. It was his wife and I said you might want to answer that now, since she will only call later and interrupt us. He answered the call and I thought oh, what is this, are men really so stupid?

His table of friends had already started drinking and were talking Farsi, since they were from Iran. He is a good looking man and I wouldn't have minded being with him, if he had been single. He was so cute, he was showing me his kids pictures -- I guess that why he wanted me there, someone to talk to and to blow up his image in front of his brother. I showed him the picture of the girls at the office and he said I should call them to come over for his friends and I said I don't mix business with pleasure. Then he and his friends started talked business again and I said just let me go up to the room and chill, because I was tired, you can come up later. . .

We were smoking cigars -- he loved it, that I smoked cigars. We were on the patio talking and it was beautiful. We actually made out on the patio and he said you are so beautiful -- he couldn't stop kissing me and kissing my hand and telling me you smell so good. The only thing I'm thinking is honey, you're not getting any. And I didn't give him any pussy either -- he just wants me to be there and to hug me and kiss me and to touch my hair and smell me -- and that's what he did, we were holding hands and kissing and smoking cigars and he was just looking at me, adoring me.

Then we both got tired and he had to get up at four in the morning. It was already midnight, so he stood up and grabbed a stack of hundreds from his shirt pocket and gave me ten of them -- a thousand bucks -- and that was when he said, what do you need my money for, if you are doing so well, so I said you can never have enough. . .

He said he had been looking forward to coming to the city because he wanted to see me . . . because I'm here. I honestly enjoying being with him because he is so smart and I learn from being around him -- he's like my mentor.

When I left he actually gave me a really long hug, a hug like he was sucking in all the love ... I wonder if he is happy with his wife. And then I just left.

And off I go, on to the next one . . .

5.

I want goodnight kisses xx

. . .

Stella's story

Come into the bedroom, I am on the bed xx. I am waiting for you. I want you. Come here to me.

Subject: Hi

Hello

Subject: Re: Hi

Hello to you too. . .

~ *A few minutes pass...*

Subject: feeling ignored, going to kitchen

Chowder is calling me. Back in a mo xx

Subject: Re: Hi

I'm back now, Scott,

xxx kisses xxx I miss you . . . Xxx Stella

Subject: RE: Hi

Well, what u up to? x Scott

Subject: What am I up to?

Now or earlier?

earlier:
--ran errands, came home, packing for trip

tomorrow:
--going out of town for New Year's Eve party
--will have the whole upstairs of my friends' house to myself (I'm sharing with the billiards table)

Come with me???!!! Xx What are you doing? Xxx Stella

Subject: RE: What am I up to?

Enjoy your party and no billiards xxx LOL. Scott

Subject: Re: What am I up to?

Okay. . .
you are quieter than usual . . .xx Stella

Subject: RE: What am I up to?

Very busy day x Scott

Subject: RE: Hi

Was just heading to bed xx Scott

Subject: Re: Hi

Oh. . .
right now???? No kisses? I want kisses. . . I missed
goodnight kisses last night xx Stella

Subject: Re: Hi

Send me a story x Scott

Subject: Re: Hi

Okay, will write one. . .give me a few minutes, okay?   It would help if you warmed me up. . .xx Stella

Subject: Re: Hi

I want to kiss u, want to suck u & want to lick u xxx Scott

Subject: Re: Hi

Oh much better now — brightening up — xx. I'll work on your story then. I tried to write something earlier today, but it didn't work out well, so that will wait. . . xx now to write your story xx Stella

Subject: Story

Scott,

I want you so much, I miss you and want your arms around me, your hands on me, your hot sweet kisses, your licking my nipples. . . (more to come) xx Stella

Subject: Re: Story

Scott,

Come into the bedroom, I am on the bed xx Stella

Subject: Re: Story

Scott,

I am waiting for you. I want you.
Come here to me, I say . . .xx Stella

Subject: RE: Story

R u naked x Scott

Subject: Re: Story

Not entirely . . .

I have on a black silk slip (which I will wear for you when you come see me) that you can see through, very sheer. Come to me and take it off. . .xx Stella

Subject: **RE: Story**

No - I want u to leave it on and feel u x Scott

Subject: **Re: Story**

Scott,

My breasts want your hands on them and my nipples want to be in your mouth . . .xxx Stella

Subject: **Re: Story**

Scott,

Come to me, now. I want you. Look, I am taking off one of the straps of the slip and my breast is out for you . . .xx Stella

Subject: **RE: Story**

I am sucking it xx

Subject: **Re: Story**

Scott,

Put your hands on my thighs and on my pussy through the sheer slip. . .xx Stella

Subject: **Re: Story**

Scott,

Put your mouth on my pussy through the slip. Inhale the smell of me. I will moan when you do. . .xx Stella

Subject: **RE: Story**

I want to lick u xx Scott

Subject: **Re: Story**

Oh lick me. . . I will go mad if you do xx . . . Oh, Scott, lick me xx Stella

Subject: RE: Story

I am licking your pussy x Scott

Subject: Re: Story

Scott,

I am so wet. I am moving my thighs and my buttocks toward your mouth. I have my hands in your hair and move them down your back xx Stella

Subject: RE: Story

Also biting your nipples x Scott

Subject: Re: Story

Oh Scott, this is so good. I am so slippery now. Let me feel your cock, your lovely hard cock. . . Xx Stella

Subject: RE: Story

I am licking you furiously x Scott

Subject: **RE: Story**

Scott,

I am so wet. I am moving my thighs and my buttocks toward your mouth. I have my hands in your hair and move them down your back xx Stella

Subject: **RE: Story**

Now I am hard xx Scott

Subject: **Re: Story**

Scott, I say, what are you going to do with that? Rub it on my breasts, rub your cock on my breasts and between them. . . xx

Subject: **RE: Story**

Your nipples are erect and I bite them harder x

Subject: **Re: Story**

Oh, Scott, you make me so hot, I will come more than once if you keep licking me like that xx Stella

Subject: **RE: Story**

I will put baby oil on your nipples and you caress my cock with them xx Scott

Subject: **Re: Story**

Oh Scott, Scott I want you. I want you . . . Stella

Subject: **RE: Story**

I want u too x Scott

Subject: **RE: Story**

Scott,

I am out of my mind. I love your slippery cock between my breasts.
Oh, you make me so hot, I will come more than once if you keep licking me like that xx Stella

Subject: RE: Story

I love licking u xx Scott

Subject: Re: Story

Scott,

I love your licking me. I love licking you. Give me your cock -- put it in my mouth xx. Stella

Subject: RE: Story

You have it now xx Scott

Subject: Fwd: Story

I roll my tongue around the head of your cock. .. I am starting to come, the first time of many, I'm sure.

I have to be very careful now . . . you are in my mouth. I inhale . . . oh oh oh xx Stella

Subject: RE: Story

Fantastic xx Scott

Subject: Re: Story

Oh my god, Scott, put your dick in my cunt while I am coming. . .xx Stella

Subject: Re: Story

Feel me come, you are so hard . . . Now ride me hard, Scott,

I want your dick -- I want your dick, I love it moving in me . . . moving hard, moving deep xx Stella

Subject: RE: Story

I am fucking you xx Scott

Subject: Re: Story

Yes and I am fucking you back, hard deep so good

Fuck me Scott fuck me xx Stella

Subject: RE: Story

I want you screaming xx Scott

Subject: Re: Story

Almost there, Scott, again, coming, almost there, I say louder and louder. . . Fuck me xx

Now I am coming again and I am shouting your name and I am screaming your name, you are so good it is so good, so good xx Stella

Subject: RE: Story

Fuck me xx Scott

Subject: **Re: Story**

*Fuck me back, fuck me . . I'll fuck you until you come
and we are drunk on each others bodies . . .xx Stella*

Subject: **RE: Story**

Are u enjoying this xxx? Scott

Subject: **Re: Story**

*Oh Scott, this is so good. I never felt this so good, so
good, fuck me until I cannot say another word . . . fuck
me until I can't think of anything else but your fucking
me . . .xx Stella*

Subject: **RE: Story**

Wow. I just came xx

Subject: **Re: Story**

Mmmm. I want to taste your come. Let me lick it off your dick xx. Stella

Subject: **RE: Story**

Lick me xxx Scott

Subject: **Re: Story**

Slurping, licking your come, so delicious. . . mmm
My pussy is so full of you and on fire at the same time. . .
Happy pussy. Very very good . . .xx Stella

Subject: **RE: Story**

I love fucking you xxx Scott

Subject: **Re: Story**

I love fucking you too xx Stella

Subject: **RE: Story**

Sweet dreams x Scott

Subject: **Re: Story**

. . . and sweet dreams to you, hot sexy man xx Stella

Subject: **RE: Story**

I would like a really hot horny story to wake up to xx Scott

Subject: **Re: Story**

I will work on that . . . nice hot story for you so you can think horny thoughts about me as I fly out of town on the plane tomorrow . . . Xxx xxx Stella xxx

6.

Back again

. . .

Regina's story

You're missing me, aren't you, he
replied . . .
Across the chasms of distance and time

After the tiff

Come take my hand, he said, I know you've missed me. . .
Step back on the roller coaster
And my heart starts to pound...addiction...withdrawal
Addiction...withdrawal...we all know where this will lead

I love the chase -- I love it . . .
The fire rages in my blood, my heart pounds
Harder, faster, the pounding in my eardrums deafens me
The pulsing behind my knees nearly drops me to the floor

Deep breath -- deep breath, as I breathe more rapidly
I am ready, I am ready for this, I want it. . .
I can feel the heat rushing through my genitals
My heart beat, my heart beat, pounding hot

Come take my hand, he says,
As the fire rages through every part of me
Come to me, he says, holding out his hand,
And I look at my hand as I start to reach out for his. . .

~*A few months have passed*

Subject: Hi

I hope all is well with you x

Ryan

Subject: Re: Hi

A message signed with an x...mmm

I am fine, mostly very busy.

Sitting in the terminal, waiting to return home after a long day out of town for a meeting.

I'm part of a dance group now -- we'll be dancing outside in town tomorrow evening - something to do with promoting some cause or another.

Been practicing. . .

Should be on YouTube.

I hope all is well with you also and things have settled down a bit. . .

Here's an x back - it was good to hear from you.

~ Regina x

~Several days later

Subject: Photos

Ryan,

Here's a photo taken after our dance performance.

It's also on YouTube, but I'm not in frame in the video.

I'm in the purple top on right -- I left the rehearsal early (10PM that night) before they decided to wear all black.

~ Regina x

Subject: Re: Photos

You look good x

Ryan

~Several minutes later, after no reply

Wow xxx

Ryan

Subject: Re: Photo

You know, Ryan, I just don't know what to say . . .

~ Regina

Subject: Re: Photos

??

Subject: Re: Photos

Well, maybe thanks for the kind words.

~ Regina

Subject: Re: Photos

As always x

Ryan

Subject: Re: Photos

Okay, then.

How have you been?

~ Regina

Subject: Re: Photos

Ok, thank you x

Ryan

Subject: Re: Photos

Where are you?

~ Regina

Subject: Re: Photos

Back in Scotland . . . alone in a bed

Ryan

Subject: Re: Photos

Ahhh...

Subject: Re: Photos

And horny x

Ryan

Subject: Re: Photos

Yes. . .

Of course. . .

~ Regina

~After a pause and inhaling a deep breath

Subject: Re: Photos

Ryan,

Try telling me you miss me or something like that.

It doesn't have to be real.

~ Regina

Subject: Re: Photos

I miss your kiss and your breasts and your bum x

Ryan

Subject: Re: Photos

Sigh. . .

Oh, okay . . .

This could be better . . .

~ Regina

Subject: Re: Photos

Ryan,

Let's start at the beginning . . .

What would you do to me if I were in bed with you right now?

I've just gotten in bed and I am sliding over next to you, but I'm not sure about this . . .

Change my mind.

~ Regina

Subject: Re: Photos

Where are you? xx

Ryan

Subject: Re: Photos

I'm at home.

It's just gone 7PM here and it's still light outside.

~ Regina

Subject: Re: Photos

I would kiss the back of your neck as you snuggle your buttocks against me and I would play with your nipples x
Ryan

Subject: Re: Photos

What would you do? x

Ryan

Subject: Re: Photos

Mmmm . . .

I move my bum so it presses against your cock.

I breathe in deeply.

I relax and make my body more open to you. . .

I'm not horny yet, but I am warming to you. . .

~ Regina

Subject: Re: Photos

As you move your bum closer I continue to kiss your neck and play with your nipples with one hand the other searches for your clit xxx

Ryan

Subject: **Photos**

Before you get to my clit, I need some gentle touching, some long, sensuous strokes up my legs and my back and around my breasts.

I want you to make me want you.

I want you to show me how much you want me, so I can get hot for you, so hot that I don't think of anything else but your skin against mine, your hard cock against my thighs, and your tongue, kissing me deep inside my pussy . .

Show me how much you want me

~ Regina

Subject: **Re: Photos**

I stroke your back and gently rub oil on your breasts xx

Ryan

Subject: **Re: Photos**

Twist my nipples. . . pinch them xxx

Subject: Re: Photos

I have sucked your nipples into my mouth and am nibbling them x

Subject: Re: Photos

I'm getting wet . . .

I want your mouth on my clit, sucking it.

I want your tongue in my pussy, licking it, sucking it deeply . . .

I am moving my pussy towards your mouth and back.

~ Regina

Subject: Re: Photos

I love kissing your pussy and licking you and biting the inside of your thighs x

Ryan

Subject: Re: Photos

Kiss and lick my inner thighs, Ryan, don't bite them.

Instead, I want you to bite the bottom of my bum cheeks, the soft underneath part where it meets my legs -- you will make me moan if you do.

Then tell me where your cock is . . .   I want to feel it.

I want to hold your golden haired balls in my hand.

~ Regina

Subject: RE: Photos

My cock is in my hand and what are you doing x

Ryan

Subject: Re: Photos

Your cock is in MY hand, Ryan, and I am caressing it . . . so hard, so lovely and large and hard, I want it. . .

I want your cock . . .

~ Regina

Subject: **RE: Photos**

My cock is in front of your pussy, you hold it and play x

Ryan

Subject: **Re: Photos**

I move the head of your cock next to my hot wet pussy, so very slippery. . .

I want you inside me, Ryan, but tease me first. . .

~Regina

Subject: **Re: Photos**

I have a huge hard on xxx I want you xx I want to fuck you x

Ryan

Subject: Re: Photos

My clit is pulsing . . .

My pussy wants you so much . . .

I want to fuck you too.

~ Regina

Subject: Re: Photos

Put your hard cock next to my cunt.

If you put the head of your cock next to my clit, you will drive me wild.

I want you to push the head of your cock next to my hot hot pussy -- it's so wet. . .

~ Regina

Subject: Hot!

Slide inside, Ryan . . . slide inside me.

~ Regina

Subject: Re: Hot!

Call now?

Ryan

Subject: Re: Hot!

Oh yes, yes, Ryan!

Call me now. . .

~ Regina

~ Ten minutes later

Subject: Re: Hot!

Ryan!

What happened?

I can't hear you.

CALL BACK!!!

~ Regina

Subject: **Re: Hot!**

Lost you

Ryan

Subject: **Re: Hot!**

Call back!

Ryan!

Call back!

Did you come?

Tell me if you came . . .

Or call me back so we can both come.

~ Regina

Subject: Dangling

Oh. At least say goodnight . . .

~ Regina

~ *Regina, thinking to herself*

Burned again. . .

Ryan, you are such a selfish prick, so many empty words have rolled off your honeyed tongue for so long.

Thank you for taking me to the edge, then leaving me dangling.

Thank you so much for that. . .

~*A day or so later*

Subject: RE: Dangling

Sorry — had broadband issues, just back now x

Ryan

~*After no answer*

Subject: RE: Dangling

Are you there? x

Ryan

Subject: Re: Dangling

I'm at the office, Ryan.

I've gone to work.

~ Regina

~*A few minutes later*

Subject: Re: Dangling

Ryan, You can be quite selfish, don't think I haven't noticed. (I like that in a man).

I'll get you back, of course ...(LOL)

~ Regina x

Subject: Re: Dangling

Ooops... LOL xxx Ryan

7.

The shoe man

. . .

Roxy's story

We were at dinner eating spaghetti puttanesca -- which means whore-like spaghetti -- that cracked me up -- I mean, how fitting ...

So me and this shoe man met last November. I mean, I was kind of attracted to him, but he liked my girlfriend, so that was a NO for me, but then, they ended up not talking, so-o-o . . .

He told me later on, after -- well, I'll get to that part in a minute -- he told me that he had tried to contact me on Facebook and I said oops, I guess I was too busy.

In June, months after I met him, my girlfriend and I went to New York City on Sunday and we stayed at his house. She and I shared the bedroom, while he slept on the couch, very gentleman-like. He gave each of us a pair of sexy shoes that he'd made -- he said he likes to see sexy shoes on sexy women. We were up talking about all kinds of stuff after we arrived that night, way on up until six the next morning. We made omelets for a late night -- early morning meal and then we went to bed. The next day -- really, later on that same day -- we got up and put on sexy cute dresses and really high high heels. He was like, damn, and we said, we'll see you later, and he was like, damn but you are staying in my house . . .

While we were in the city, we met three different guys in three different spots and ate three different times,

back to back, after we first met with the Jewish jeweler
and looked at diamonds and pearls.

Guy #1 was in his late 20's. He was a Russian
model who gets paid about $5k a day for a shoot. He
picked us up in a BMW. We went out for some oysters,
salad, and wine -- we had a good time talking. My
girlfriend and I were adoring him and drooling when we
looked at him, because he was so freaking hot and had a
nonchalant Russian way about him -- even when he was
cursing, it sounded hot.

Then we met Guy #2 in the meat packing district --
he took us to a spot on 9th avenue that had a cute little
garden with green leaves in the back. We had appetizers
and a couple of drinks -- it was pretty nice. Guy #2
works for a pharmaceutical company and he talked about
how he wants to make sure people don't contract HIV.
He told us about the importance of using dental dams and
I was like OMG because the night before, I sucked the
dick of this hot guy I'd been seeing -- I sucked his dick
and swallowed his come and now, OMG, I could get, um,
OMG . . .

After that, we went to spot #3, which was an Italian
restaurant with Guy #2 and Guy #3 showed up -- these
guys were all my girlfriend's guys, I did not know them
until now. While we were at dinner, we were eating
spaghetti puttanesca, which means whore-like spaghetti.

That cracked me up, whore-like spaghetti -- I was thinking, how fitting. Meanwhile, the shoe guy was trying to reach us to ask us when were we coming home, meaning back to his place, so we finished dinner and started back to shoe guy's place. My girlfriend and I were laughing like crazy in the cab on the way back, because the cab driver who picked us up was the same cab driver from the night before.

By the time we got back, my girlfriend decided she wanted to see Guy #2, so she asked me if it was okay for me to stay with the shoe guy by myself that night. I said oh, it's no problem, but he's going to be mad at you, because you're leaving for some other ding-a-ling and you didn't give him any pussy. My girlfriend texted Guy #2 to say she was coming over that night, then we had to explain to the shoe man that she was going to leave. He said how did you know that I was okay with this? She was like, well I'm leaving you company and we both started laughing. Later he told me he was actually pretty happy about her leaving, because he thought I was really hot earlier that day when he saw me in my sexy little dress. Now he calls my girlfriend Miss Pimp-alicous, like a pimp, because she left me behind with him so she could leave his house for another dude.

After she left, he was very concerned about making me comfortable and asked I what wanted to do. I told him that I thought we could talk and watch the movie, so we went to the store to get some pineapple-orange juice to drink. To my surprise, he also bought some cookie dough. He made cookies from the dough, then put them in the oven and baked them while he was taking a shower. When he came out, the cookies were a little burnt, but he still brought me cookies and milk. It was so cute -- I said that's okay, the cookies are only a little crisp, so we had burnt cookies and milk.

We started watching the movie -- I don't even remember the name of it -- and he made me lie next to him, under his arm with my legs stretched out on the right side. He started rubbing my head and I breathed out a sigh because I was starting to relax. Then he started caressing my skin and I thought, oh my god, I'm getting hot, so I put the cover down -- I was wearing a little nightgown. Then he took my left hand and started licking my fingers -- sucking on my fingers -- and I thought, oh shit. Then he started kissing my head, while I was just like trying to focus on the movie.

I guess he got tired of waiting while I watched the movie, so he started whispering that he just wanted to kiss me all night, all over, all night, all over. He had this firm, but gentle touch. He was grabbing me, but not too hard and not too soft, and I knew he just wanted me -- I mean, I don't know what it is about these guys -- they just love my body so much, they can't have enough. . .

So anyway, he was kissing my legs and right between my panty lines, not on the panty itself, but right on the lines. He kept on just teasing and teasing . . . He pulled the panties to the side to get to my vagina, then he stopped again and came up and kissed me on the mouth. He said he just wanted to kiss me, as he took my glasses off.

He kissed me all the way up my arms, kissed my nipples, and kissed my belly button too, as he took my panties off. He started licking me all over -- front, back, side to side -- just licking, sucking, and sticking his tongue in. He got me so horny and so wet, that I came. Then he started on me again. . . He moved me a little to the side, so he was on the floor and I was on the couch and kept kissing me and licking me until he made me come again. He kept telling me how good I tasted -- I said I know, I can taste myself on your lips when you kiss me on the mouth.

He turned me around, took my nightdress off, and arranged me so we were positioned doggie style. He kept all his clothes on and dry humped me. I could feel his big dick against my butt -- and he was huge. He licked my butt cheeks, then licked my anus and stuck his tongue in, while he was playing with my clit.

Then he pushed me up so I had my hands on the back of the couch and told me to go to the bedroom and play with myself, because he had to go someplace. I said what, why? He said not to ask him -- he had to go out to get something. Ask me, I said, ask me if I have what you have to go get, so he asked me if I had any condoms. Of course I did, because I don't want to get any diseases, so I got the condoms out, hoping they would fit him -- I mean, he was huge. I said you are a single man, you should always be prepared, He said that was not his priority right now, meaning sex, I guess -- interesting, huh.

He didn't even put the condom on -- he just went down on me and made me come again. By now, I was soaked. I told him OMG you drive me crazy. I ripped the condom package open with my teeth, placed the condom on the tip of his dick, and rolled it down the shaft of his dick with my mouth. Then he slid his dick in my pussy -- he slid in really slowly and gently. He was stroking me and telling me in his deep sexy voice that he wanted to get to know my body from the beginning to the end of it, every bit. He started by saying he loved my lips and my neck and my nipples -- with each stroke he was telling me a different part of my body that he loved. I enjoyed it very much, his dick was filling me up, fulfilling me, you know what I mean?

He turned me around and said I should tell him how I want it, so he could hit the right spot and make me feel good. Then before I knew what was happening, his dick was out of my coochie and his mouth licking my juices, like he had been thirsty for days. He made love to each part of my body, so he could take it all in. I came again, so he turned me around and we did missionary style this time. He was stroking deeper and deeper, asking me how it felt. I answered him with each stroke, so good, so good, so good . . .

Now he came -- I felt him pulsing inside me and it turned me on. He pulled me so close and hugged me, so I could feel his heart beating so fast. He asked me if I knew that he wanted me. I said I knew that from the first time I met him. He lay on his back and pulled me closer to him, wrapping his arm around me and our legs were interwoven. He took my left hand, placed it on his chest, right where his heart was and we fell asleep.

In the morning, we woke up together and he started kissing me again. I thought eeuhh, I have morning breath, oh well, fuck it -- I enjoyed him too much to worry about that. He got under the covers and started licking me again, then he grabbed the condom, put it on, and we started fucking again.

This time he was talking about the things that he was going to do to me the next time we saw each other. He said he was going to lick my pussy and lick my butt, and have anal sex with me. He said he wants to feel me come and see how nasty I am. He said he wants me to remember his dick inside me when I am on my way home. He stroked me deeper and deeper and we held each other so tight, sweating all over each other. All I was thinking was, oh yeah, I want to feel you like that.

We kissed and came together, so hard, really really hard. We lay there for a minute, catching our breath. Then he pulled his dick out of my coochie and kissed my tattoo, high up on my thigh. I told him, you are a good instrument player after all. . .

When I left in the morning, I was wearing the sexy shoes he gave me. Thanks for the cookies and the milk, daddy. . .

8.

Oily Sunday morning

. . .

Regina's story

Wherever you are, find me. . . I want to fuck you like crazy.

Subject: **Good morning**

Good morning, Ryan.

Waking up. Making a pot of tea.

Xxx Regina

Subject: **Re: Good morning**

Are you still overseas?

I'm at work, wishing your long tongue were flicking my clit.

Xxx Regina

Subject: **RE: Good morning**

Yes I'm still in Europe - that is a nice thought with my tongue x

Ryan

Subject: **Re: Good morning**

I wish my tongue were licking your golden haired balls

Xxx Regina

Subject: **RE: Good morning**

That would be nice - then I could come in your mouth xx

Ryan

Subject: **Re: Good morning**

Yes yes yes I love it when you do. . .

You taste sooo good

Like seaspray and sunshine . . .

~ Regina

Subject: **RE: Good morning**

What would you like me to do x

Ryan

Subject: Re: Good morning

Mmmm can't think straight ... Wish I could take my clothes off and were in bed with you

I want to drag my tits down your chest till they reach your crouch and run my nipples through your pubic hair -- then I want you to suck my clit and drive me wild with your fingers inside my cunt

Xxx Regina

Subject: RE: Good morning

Yum - very descriptive xx

Ryan

Subject: Re: Good morning

I am very wet right now... Over to you

Xxx Regina

Subject: **RE: Good morning**

Are you sitting down? If so I would place my head between your legs and lick your clit and bite the inside of your thigh x

Ryan

Subject: **Re: Good morning**

Oooooo yes nice - I couldn't stand up if I tried ... (Pulsing)

Xxx Regina

Subject: **RE: Good morning**

As I am licking you I would fuck you with my fingers xx and fondle your breasts xx

Ryan

Subject: **Re: Good morning**

My clit is throbbing
My pussy is flooded it's so wet
My breasts will follow your fingers anywhere xx
Is your horn standing up?
I want to feel it hard against my thighs...

Xxx Regina

Subject: **RE: Good morning**

Yes I am very hard xxxx

Ryan

Subject: **Re: Good morning**

I love it when you put your hard cock between my thighs
with the tip just grazing my clit and rest it my pubic hair
I'm crazy hot for your dick
Kiss me deep and hard
Put your tongue alongside mine inside my mouth and kiss
me ...

Xxx Regina

Subject: **RE: Good morning**

I love kissing you xx

Ryan

Subject: **Re: Good morning**

Xxx Regina mmmmmmm

~Later, that night

Subject: **RE: Good morning**

You there x

Ryan

~Later, a few hours past midnight

Subject: **Re: Good morning**

Ryan,

Are you really awake at 3AM UK time? Or are you back in US? Fell asleep very early tonight -- had a wee (!) bit of champers at a party.

Awake now (2AM), ha ha. And very horny for you, too, wherever you are. Find me, I want to fuck you like crazy.

Xxx Regina

~Later, after sunrise

Subject: **RE: Good morning**

Have a huge hot horn xx

Ryan

Subject: **Re: Good morning**

Oooo, let's not waste it. . .

Xxx Regina

Subject: RE: Good morning

I am rubbing oil on it x

Ryan

Subject: Re: Good morning

I could do that ... I love holding your dick . . . let's see, oil on your dick, oops, spilled some on me...

Xxx Regina

Subject: RE: Good morning

I could rub it into your breasts x

Ryan

Subject: **Re: Good morning**

I like that, oily breasts. . . I'll rub them on your chest, then turn over -- I'll rub them on your buttocks, while I stroke your dick and trace my oily fingers around your balls. . .

Xxx Regina

Subject: **RE: Good morning**

Now getting harder xx

Ryan

Subject: **Re: Good morning**

mmm mmm mmm . . .

I think I will lick your bum and then put my head through your thighs and lick your balls . . .

Nice . . .

~Regina

Subject: **Re: Good morning**

I am rubbing harder -- very horny xx

Ryan

Subject: **Re: Good morning**

You have my pussy and clit throbbing for you.

We are lying on our sides, reverse spoons and I am on the outside with my head through your thighs. Now I slither up a bit and run my tongue up your shaft . . .Xxx R

~Regina

Subject: **Re: Good morning**

I reach the top of your cock and run my tongue around the tip of your penis. Then I suck it in my mouth...

~Regina

Subject: **RE: Good morning**

I am going to come -- would you like me to lick you? xx

Ryan

Subject: **Re: Good morning**

Yes, come in my mouth, then lick me until I come for you ...

Xxx Regina

Subject: **RE: Good morning**

I am about to come xx

Ryan

Subject: **RE: Good morning**

I am rubbing hard now xxx

Ryan

Subject: Re: Good morning

Give me your come... I want your hot come in my mouth, fill it up...so good . . .

~Regina

Subject: RE: Good morning

I want to fuck x

Ryan

Subject: Re: Good morning

Me too - I want to fuck you - fuck me

I want you really really badly

I want you to fuck me xx

~Regina

Subject: Re: Good morning

Give me your dick. . . fuck me... Stick your dick inside me and fuck me xx

~ Regina

Subject: RE: Good morning

Wow. Just came xx

Ryan

Subject: Re: Good morning

Oooo good...

~ Regina

Subject: Re: Good morning

Wet

Very wet

Hot for you

Hot for your tongue..

Hot for your mouth on my pussy

~ Regina

Subject: **RE: Good morning**

Tell me when you come x

Ryan

Subject: **Re: Good morning**

Very hot

Very hot....

Getting close xxx

~ Regina

Subject: **Re: Good morning**

Oooooo -- catching breath -- that was hot! very nice . . .
Xx

~ Regina

Subject: RE: Good morning

Great -- speak soon xxxx

Ryan

Subject: Re: Good morning

Mmmm . . .

Lovely morning, kisses for that xxx

Xxx Regina

9.

The meeting at the office

. . .

Stella's story

We were in a meeting today. Suddenly, I imagined I saw you in front of me, then I definitely felt your dick thrust deep inside me.

Subject: Remember that mistletoe?

Scott,

Remember Christmas morning, when I got up at 4AM, climbed up a step ladder and snipped the mistletoe to hold it over my pussy and dream of your hot kisses? I brought all the snippy bits of the mistletoe back with me, waiting for those kisses, hot kisses, waiting for you.

Last night, after you went to bed, I made lots of little meat pies -- I do this every year, the first week in January. It was getting quite late, so I put on some electronic dance music, to make the three hours in the kitchen lively - I usually like classical music or jazz, but the dance music was really good, in more ways than one. There was a very low pulsing, bass line that went right up from the soles of my feet, straight to my pussy, and made it throb all evening. When I finished with the pies, very very late (early in the AM) I started writing for you and the bass line with the pulsing music worked its way into your good morning story. . .

That beat makes me want to come come come -- I'll make you come . . . I'll make you come. . .

I was hot for you off and on all day today. Come make hot sweet love to me, Scott, come make hot love to me.

Mmmm. xx

Look at this photo and see me climbing up a step ladder at 4AM in the pitch dark, with the pouring rain against the skylights above, with my nipples tightening wanting you, and snipping off the mistletoe to hold over my pussy, wanting your kisses . . .

~x o x o x~ Stella

~ *Later that morning*

Subject: **Today**

Scott,

I want you . . .

I was sitting in staff meeting a few hours ago when I suddenly felt you thrust your dick inside me . .

It was very vivid.

Felt wonderful so very good. . .

Had a hard time maintaining my facial expression

~ xx Stella

~ *Later that evening*

Subject: RE: Today

You are a horny lady - am in bed x

Scott

Subject: Re: Today

All your fault -- I want to get in bed with you (taking off clothes)

~xx Stella

Subject: RE: Today

That would be lovely xx Scott

Subject: Re: Today

Mmmm,

Put your arms around me and pull me over to you, then put your hands around my breasts.

Are you still coming to see me?

~ Xx Stella

Subject: Re: Today

(waiting, waiting, waiting . . .)

I obviously need to turn up heat on my red hot oven . . .

~Xx Stella

Subject: RE: Today

That feels good and yes am trying to arrange that xx

Scott

Subject: Re: Today

Okay, I'll be very good and not remind you all the time how much my pussy wants you inside . . .

~Xx Stella

Subject: Re: Today

However . . .

It was indescribably hot today during a meeting at work. How did that happen? All of a sudden, I felt you inside me and moved (managed not to moan). . .

Mmm. . .

~xx Stella

Subject: RE: Today

Sorry bad Internet connection tell me more xx

Scott

Subject: Re: Today

Ah,

We were in a routine meeting after the holidays. Just before my turn to speak, I suddenly could see you in front of me and definitely felt your dick thrust deep inside me. One thrust. Out of nowhere. I almost came. I was shocked. It felt really good - really really good. My body jerked up straight, sitting up in the chair and I had to uncross my legs and take a deep breath. Wow.

After the meeting, I went back to check if you had sent me a horny message (no), so I don't know where that came from, but it was really good. Made me want you more, if that is even possible.

~Xx Stella

Subject: RE: Today

Can't wait to lick your pussy xxx

Scott

Subject: Re: Today

Oh yes, please.

I'm still trembly from thinking about today, earlier at work. . .

Scott, that was amazing.

Lick my pussy. . .

~xx Stella

Subject: RE: Today

Tell me what else you want as I begin fondling your breasts x

Scott

Subject: Re: Today

I have been simmering just below boiling, for days now, wanting you.

It's really nice, like being on the brink of coming all the time.

What do I taste like?

~Xx Stella

Subject: RE: Today

You taste wonderful - very sweet x

Scott

Subject: Re: Today

I want to keep feeling this hot . . .

Right now, flick your tongue around my cunt, then go down on my clit . . .

Ah h h h. . .

Where are your hands . . .

~Xx Stella

Subject: RE: Today

My hands are on my balls xx

I begin nibbling your clit x

Scott

Subject: Re: Today

I love your balls . . .

I want to lick the hairy parts of your balls

Move, curve around me so I can feel your pubic hair on my tongue . . .

Put your whole mouth around my clit (don't bite) and suck hard . . .

~xx Stella

Subject: RE: Today

You will come too soon xxx

Scott

Subject: Re: Today

Ah, if I do come, it won't the the only time tonight . . .

Oh Scott, this is too good.

I lick around your balls and under them, just above your anus

~xx Stella

Subject: RE: Today

Yum xxx

Love that x

Want you xx

Scott

Subject: RE: Today

I am now stroking my cock with baby oil xx

Scott

Subject: Re: Today

Oooooo. . .

What will you do with it, your oily cock?

~Xx Stella

Subject: Re: Today

I like to rub my breasts over your cock and your balls and let my nipples tingle

~xx Stella

Subject: RE: Today

I turn you around and tease your anus with the tip of my cock and fondle your breasts xx

Scott

Subject: Re: Today

Oooo, nice. . .

Get me really hot, get my pussy really hot, and we'll see what happens in back . . .

~Xx Stella

Subject: RE: Today

As I bite the back of your neck x

Scott

Subject: Re: Today

I love that . . .

Bite more. . .

Bite once sharply. . .

Make me jump with pleasure (like you did today earlier)

~xx Stella

Subject: RE: Today

I finger you as I tease you xx

Scott

Subject: Re: Today

Oh oh oh,

Now my palms are tingling,

My thighs are tingling

And I am feeling like I could come . . .

~xx Stella

Subject: Re: Today

Now I want you inside my cunt as I come,

As I come . . .

I am coming

~xx Stella

Subject: RE: Today

As you are coming, I bite and pull your hair and massage your head — still teasing you xx

Scott

Subject: Re: Today

(wild moans)

xx I'm trying not to scratch you.

I press my fingers in your back,

Then in your head,

Then in your back again

And rub them up and down your torso

~xx Stella

Subject: Re: Today

My toes are curling. . .

Oh so good, Scott. . .

You are — oh — so good

~xx Stella

Subject: RE: Today

As I stroke harder I am looking at a pic of you x

Scott

Subject: Re: Today

Which picture?

Which one?

I love this xx

I am vain.

I love your looking at me.

I love looking at you.

I love looking at your cock, your beautiful cock.

You make me so hot.

~Xx Stella

Subject: RE: Today

The one of you in the games room on New Year's Eve xx

I want to come on you xx

Scott

Subject: Re: Today

Yes, come on me. . .

I want your sperm on me. . .

On my breasts. . .

On my face. . .

In my hair . . .

~Xx Stella

Subject: RE: Today

I am imaging what your pussy looks like as I sit over you stroking my cock as you play x

Scott

Subject: Re: Today

My pussy is hot and wet and dark around the lips, tinged with pink and wanting your tongue to lick it . . .

~Xx Stella

Subject: RE: Today

I want to see your pussy tonight xx

Scott

Subject: Re: Today

You'll see it again soon . . .

You'll like the inside of my pussy best of all. . .

Mmm. . .

I want to see a picture of your cock xx

~xx Stella

Subject: Re: Today

Your cock will snuggle right up inside my pussy and make itself at home . . .

~Xx Stella

Subject: RE: Today

Sent photo xx

Scott

Subject: Re: Today

? No photo yet . . .

~Xx Stella

Subject: RE: Today

Sent from work phone

Didn't go xx

It was a pic of my cock x

Scott

Subject: Re: Today

Your work phone?

Are you serious?

Ooh, you are so wicked. . .

I want to see your cock. . .

~Xxx Stella

Subject: RE: Today

Coming in a minute . . .

Looking at your photo xx

Scott

Subject: Re: Today

Come on me xx

I want to lick your sperm

~xxx Stella

Subject: Fwd: Today

I love how you taste. . .

Are you coming?

~Xx Stella

Subject: RE: Today

Wow xx

Scott

Subject: Re: Today

xx Wow here too xx

I still want a picture of your cock.

I must have a lovely cock piccie

~xx Stella

Subject: RE: Today

Now I will sleep well xx

goodnight xx

Scott

Subject: Re: Today

Sweet dreams, hot sexy Scott,

Kisses too xxx. . .

But don't think I've forgotten . . .

I still want a picture of your cock to see in my dreams

~xx Stella

10.

All the dessert you need

. . .

Marilyn's story

When we ordered dessert, he laughed and said, "I'm all the chocolate you need . . ."

I told him he would have to take the consequences for his actions. . . I told him that when he took me out to dinner, he dropped me off at my apartment when the evening was over, waited in the parking lot a while, then he came back to have sex with me. Now he's texting me all the time and coming over to my office . . .

You know, I think he is -- taking the consequences, that is. He always tells me I would be the one if this were a different time and place and if he weren't separated and still married. He's supposed to be getting divorced . . . he's been separated since last November, but who knows if he's going through with it. I'm honored to be around you, that's what he always says.

He called me and asked what are you doing later? I said I'm at work and he said when are you off? I said 7:30 and he said he'd pick me up at 8 and that he said he wanted it to be just me, one on one, not to bring anyone else -- he meant don't bring anyone of my girlfriends, like I usually do. He wanted tonight to be special -- just one on one time, just us.

So we went to a place that was really romantic -- there was a candle on the table and I asked him if he picked this restaurant on purpose. I thought ahhh . . . our first romantic date.

Dinner was delicious. I had fish, potatoes, vegetables, salad and I had this lobster bisque soup to start. . . It was really good. You know he's a big guy, so he ate a lot. He had salad, soup, bread and something I don't remember for dinner. We ordered dessert -- there was strawberry cheesecake, fresh fruit tart, and a three layer chocolate cake. He laughed when we were choosing dessert. He said I'm all the chocolate that you need . . . We stayed there talking and flirting until we were the last people in the restaurant and he paid the bill.

He wanted to meet some of his guy friends at the bar and show me off -- he was on a high, being with me. We had a beer and I was dancing and he actually danced too -- a tall black man dancing salsa, can you picture it? And then I said we do have to talk, because I didn't know what was going on with his marriage, separation, and divorce. He said what do we have to talk about and I said you know what, because I need to know what's going on with your marriage and do you have a date when you will be divorced? He said I have only been separated since November. I asked him was that why we only exchanged numbers on the third time we met? That's when I asked him if he knows what he's getting himself into and he needs to be fully aware of the consequences of his actions. I said I don't want anyone to get hurt or fall in love or something like that and he said he was fully aware of that. I just thought we'd keep it this way and we'd just be friends or whatever.

I was getting tired and wanted to get home anyway, so we left and he dropped me off at my car, of course opening the car door, like the gentleman he is. He gave me a kiss and said he'd meet me at my house and I said you can't really do that and that he knows that -- I just keep him moving . . .

So I went home to take a shower and call my other guy, the really hot one who lives out of town by the beach, but this guy called three or four times while I was in the shower, then he sent me a text message saying he was waiting in the parking lot. I thought WTF, it was already 1:30 in the morning. . .

Then I thought, so what -- I don't have a ring on my finger. . .

I told him sorry, I was in the shower and he said I wanted to give you time. . . So I gave him a towel and wash cloth -- I don't want him in my bed not having taken a bath all day. After his shower, he started caressing me and gave me a massage with baby oil and was admiring my body. He said OMG, your body is so beautiful. . . And the only thing I'm thinking is that this dude does not know what he is getting himself into.

So he went down on me and was kissing me again. After the massage, I was already relaxed, so he made me horny. Then he put the oil all over my body and we had sex -- but you know a couple of times, his dick just kept getting smaller and he had to stroke it to get it bigger. He flipped me around and looked at my butt and he sighed and said OMG. I guess he liked what he was looking at. . . He started grabbing my hips and caressing my back while he was stroking himself. He was moaning -- he's a loud moaner. . .

Since he was having trouble staying hard, I played with myself so we could come at the same time. When we did, he got up and went into the bathroom. I said I'm done and he said are you kicking me out? I said I told you had to be prepared for the consequences of your actions. I laughed and turned around so I could go to sleep, hugging my pillow cause I don't want him to get attached. Of course he started spooning. It was so funny -- giving him the cold shoulder made him want more of me . . . much more.

In the morning he woke me up and pulled the covers down and started licking my pussy again. He was admiring my body and said it was even better with the lights on. He was touching me all over -- he has big hands and I felt so small under him. Hmmm. . . this chocolate man made me feel so good.

Now you know I'm not really a morning person . . . we did it again and he wanted me to get on top of him. I did for a little while, but I was just too tired and told him to get back on top, so he could finish.

When he left, I went back to sleep. He said I wish I had your life and I said a lot of people do. I said I'll see you next week and he said really? I said I'm going on vacation, I don't have time, and he needs to understand that. He said that he did understand. I said awww, are you going to miss me?

He said he wanted to drop me off at the airport and pick me up, which was cool with me -- that means I don't have to drive...I just had to make sure that he didn't know I was going away for the week with my other guy...

And off -- he is gone -- I'm on to the next one. . .

11.

An unexpected day off

. . .

Regina's story

"I was dressed too, but I went back to my hotel room and I'm lying on the bed, naked

Subject: **Good morning**

Hi v horny for you xx

Ryan

Subject: **Re: Good morning**

Very horny too

Want to fuck you but have to go to a meeting in a min

Wish you had been horny when I woke up a few hours ago -- I really wanted to fuck you then -- Still do

Lick me under the table. . . Make me wet and my nipples pucker

Xxx Regina

Subject: **RE: Good morning**

I would love to lick you under the table xxx

Ryan

Subject: **Re: Good morning**

Mmmmmm

I'm going to imagine your tongue in my cunt xxx

Sooo hot for you

Xxx Regina

~ *The next day*

Subject: **Re: Good morning**

Ryan,

Are you awake? I want you to fuck me. I'm crazy horny for you, hot.

If you are asleep, I could suck you awake and you could come in my mouth, mmmmm. Then we could fuck later . . .

Xxx Regina

Subject: **Re: Good morning**

Hi x

Ryan

Subject: **??**

I have an unexpected day off work and I am at home
today. There's a strange situation at the office, so
the building has been shut down for the day.

Subject: **RE: ??**

**Hi am in US in New England today - then to
midwest x**

Ryan

Subject: **RE: ??**

xx Horny for you xx

~ Regina

Subject: **RE: ??**

Are you at work LOL x

Ryan

Subject: **RE: ??**

No, at home. A fire at the office early this morning shut down my building, so we have an unexpected day off today xxx

~ Regina xxx

Subject: **RE: ??**

Ryan, I want to suck you xxx

~ Regina x

Subject: **RE: ??**

That would be wonderful x I could take out my cock x

Ryan

Subject: **RE: ??**

Yes take it out. I want it. I want it in my mouth xx

~ Regina xxx

Subject: **RE: ??**

Are you still in bed xx

Ryan

Subject: **RE: ??**

No, Ryan, I was dressed for work, then I got call about the fire when I was walking out the door. But -- I have taken off my dress and my panties and I am taking off my bra right now... xxx hot wet xxx and I want you xxx

~ Regina x

Subject: RE: ??

I was dressed too - went back to room when I heard from you x

I have a half an hour x

Ryan

Subject: RE: ??

Suck my nipples xx

~ Regina xxx

Subject: RE: ??

Would you like me to bite them x

Ryan

Subject: RE: ??

Yes yes yes xx

~ Regina x

Subject: RE: ??

I am on lying on the hotel bed naked xx

Ryan

Subject: FWD: ??

I love your cock in my mouth.

My nipples are hard xx

~ Regina xxx

Subject: RE: ??

I am on top of you, Ryan, and I am kissing you, starting with your mouth, then your neck, then your nipples, then your belly and NOW I am down at your cock xxx

~ Regina x

Subject: **FWD: ??**

Oh lovely, I say and run my tongue around your cock xx

~ Regina

Subject: **RE: ??**

Yum sounds great - I have a hard on xx

Ryan

Subject: **FWD: ??**

I've got your hard dick in my mouth now ...

Subject: **RE: ??**

I'm very hard now and playing xx

Ryan

Subject: **FWD: ??**

Lovely cock, rolling my tongue around it . . . my nipples are kissing your thighs xx

Subject: **RE: ??**

Love that xx

Ryan

Subject: **RE: ??**

Send me a photo x

Subject: **RE: ??**

Ok . . .

Just a minute xx

~ Regina

Subject: Photo

Here's a lovely torso pose, my hair along my breasts, just waiting for you to lick my nipples xx and put your hands around my waist and pull me close to you . . .

~ Regina xxx

Subject: RE: Photo

Yum - I would love to fuck you xx

Ryan

Subject: RE: Photo

Yes, I want your horn. I am hot and wet and want you xx CALL ME!

~ *The phone rings*

Ryan: Mmmm Hello mmmm . . . I want to fuck you. . . I want to fuck you NOW . . .

Regina: I want to fuck you too, Ryan. Put your cock into my cunt. I want you inside me, I want you, I want you. Kiss me deep and hard as you slide in. Kiss my lips, then kiss my mouth, then nibble my lips and put your tongue inside my mouth and touch my tongue, then twirl around my tongue with yours.

Regina: I am grabbing your cock with my pussy, can you feel my pussy grabbing your cock? My pussy is pulsing from the heat and electricity pulsing from you into me ... I can feel every bit of you inside me and there is electricity from you going through my cunt and all my body through my nipples. I am wrapping my legs around your torso and holding you close to me as I rock my pelvis closer to you and back again, riding your lovely long hard pole.

Regina: Tell me when you're coming, I want to know when you're coming, it turns me on when you do.

Regina: Oh. Oh. Oh . . . You're coming aren't you? You will make me come when you do.

Regina: Oh god you're good. I can feel it coming, can you feel it when I come, when my pussy starts to pulse, first slowly and gently then faster and much more tightly . . . Oh what have you done to me, I am coming now, feel me come, feel me come. . .

Ryan: Oh I love fucking you . . . ahhhh

Regina: Oh, deep breath. Oh. Oh. Oh. . .

~ After the moaning stops, there's just the sound of breathing. Then a few moments later

Ryan: I have to go now. . . off to do a day's work ...

Regina: Lovely day, mmm. . .

Ryan: Mine just got better . . . I love starting the day with you and a good morning fuck. . .

~ *A little while later*

Regina had heard people talking in the kitchen when she and Ryan were on the phone and thought it was probably the field manager and installation crew who had let themselves in to work on the remodeling project.

When she walked downstairs, she realized their voices had gotten quiet during her call with Ryan and they were now standing in the kitchen, silent, looking down at their feet, and seemed a bit sheepish. . .

Oh well, she thought. . . I really hope they didn't heard us, but they probably did.

Well, there's nothing I can do about it now . . .

12.

The second dessert

. . .

Marilyn's story

*He texted me to say, "You are going to
have more chocolate for your second
dessert of the day."   So I texted him back
and said, "I love chocolate and nuts . . ."*

He's in love . . .

He called me again on Tuesday morning after we were together Monday night and I thought he had butt dialed me, but then he started singing a love song to me and I just cracked up. It was at 10:30 AM, when he knew for a fact that was the time when I wake up, so he must have wanted me to wake up with him singing to me. Then he said he wanted to see me and I said I have time between three and four, come over to my office and steal a kiss from me.

So back to the day before, on Monday . . .

We were on the phone and I said I was hungry. He said okay let's go get lunch, that he was just two blocks away. So we were talking over lunch and that's why I was late for the afternoon meetings.

I told him one of my friends told me I would not be a good wife because I was too independent, but I would be a good mother. He told me I needed a man who understands my busy schedule.

I said ok . . . and he said what you are looking for might be right under your nose . . . and I said you are not even divorced yet, you're just separated, I want to see some papers -- I was giving him a hard time.

So when I dropped him off back at work he texted me, saying he was inside his office, so text him when I got back to the office.

We started texting each other naughty things . . .

I texted him, you should be inside something else . . . I'm driving him nuts, ha ha ha. . . I texted him I want sex, I want to extend my arms fully side by side with my ankles in each hand -- thank god for my yoga training. . .

He texted me that he was still at his office in a meeting but he would text me soon.

So I texted him thanks again for lunch, you satisfied one appetite, to be continued . . . you've got dinner and dessert, me.

He texted me you are going to have more chocolate for your second dessert of the day, me, tonight.

So I texted him that I love chocolate and nuts, what time will you be here (I wanted him to come to the office).

He texted back that he'd be sooner rather than later. . .

When he showed up at the office, he started grabbing me. I got my really high heels and put them on, so I could kiss him and not break my neck -- he's so tall . . .

I said thanks for coming. He said I'm just here to please you, so I said you just want me to use you and he said ABSOLUTELY.

So I did -- I just used him for my pleasure. He was feeling me and touching me and kissing me -- he's a very good kisser -- you'd love kissing him, he's really good.

Then he took my clothes off . . .

He pulled up my dress and saw that I didn't have anything on under it, so he pulled my dress all the way up and held my hands so I couldn't move and kissed me on my lips, then on my neck, then on my coochie -- you'd love to have sex with him, he is so sensual.

So I managed to pull up his shirt up and I took his clothes off -- this was right in the front of the big picture window at the front of my office -- you can't see through it, the picture window, it's frosted glass, but I'll bet you can see the shapes we made if you were outside looking in.

I lifted my leg up and did a ballet pose, putting it on top of the bar. He came up behind me and wrapped his arms around me and held me. So we did it while I had my leg up on the office bar. He loved it. He said oooh you are so-o-o flexible.

So after we finished having sex, we just sat down and I sat on him straddling him. We were both naked. He was kissing me and licking my neck. I had my sexy slow jam playlist that I like to play during sex and LL Cool J came on, so he started singing along with the LL Cool J song. He asked me why I let him come to my office. I said I had work to do and I needed a change of location. Then we made out some more, but by then we both were getting tired, so I said let's get dressed and go home. We each went to our own homes. He told me to text him when I got home okay, so I did. Then I texted my other guy, that hot guy that lives out of state on the beach to tell him that I was home from work.

But, like I said, he's definitely in love, singing love songs in the morning kind of love. You always want what you can't have, right?

And so, on to the next one . . . Right after I hung up from his love song singing Tuesday morning, that football player texted and said he was coming back to the city and wanted to see me. I thought, you are going to be next, football player. . .

13.

Away at the ocean beach house

. . .

Regina's story

*Lots of seafood, lots of wine. Call me xx
and wake me up, so we can have hot sex at
the beach house. . .*

Subject: **Did you call 2x or was that a mistake?**

Ryan . . .

    If so, I'm really sorry to miss you xx I'm very horny for you. I loved the hot sex in the hotel with you Wednesday xxx

    I'm leaving office early today at lunchtime for a weekend at the coast. I could have hot sex with you while at I'm at the B&B Saturday or Sunday morning, if you get horny xx

    The internet was down at home this morning — it is a major regional outage, but my cell phone works

~ xx Regina x

Subject: **FW: Did you call 2x or was that a mistake?**

    x I'm driving to ocean now xxx Regina

~*Very early the next morning*

Subject: **RE: Did you call 2x or was that a mistake?**

**Just flew back home xx jetlagged --
transatlantic jetlag at that xx**

Ryan

~ *And very late the night after that*

Subject: **Re: Did you call 2x or was that a mistake?**

Inebriated.

Midnight.

Big dinner party, lots of seafood.

Lots of wine too LOL.

Will write you Sunday morning, if I am not as hung over as I deserve to be.

I've been very horny for you all day today.

I want to fuck you (I did, actually, 2x this afternoon, after thinking about you naked in bed at that hotel. That was so-o-o hot. . .)

I love being at the coast - it's still a bit cool here by Florida standards, but very lovely & I still want your hard cock in between my breasts . . . Xx xx xx.

The WiFi connection is very spotty here (at the beach) xx

~ Regina xxx

~ *Late Sunday afternoon.*

Subject: RE: Did you call 2x or was that a mistake?

Stay horny xx

Ryan

Subject: RE: Good morning

Want to tie you up xx

**Want to suck you til you come on my face xx
and then I want to fuck you in every position xx**

Ryan

Subject: RE: Good morning

Ahhhh. . .

I tried many times xx

very late xx

goodnight talk later x

Ryan

~ And a few hours later

Subject: **Re: Good morning**

I'm just back at my house. It was a long drive back. I was so horny for you driving back. There was too much traffic, I couldn't drive faster, and it was too crowded, so I couldn't stop anywhere. . . I am so very horny for you. I wish I could have checked my emails - I would have found a way to stop, somehow, sexy man xxx.

I want to fuck you and I want you to come on my breasts after fucking me with your cock in between them and I want to suck your lovely cock. . .I want to lick your come, I want to taste it.

Xx Very very horny for you xx

~ Regina xx

Subject: **Tie me up**

Yes, oh yes please - tie me up - I'd like a bit of v sexy domination xx

Oooo ooo, yes tie me up !!! Yes! Smack my bottom, bite my nipples, fuck me and fuck me some more. I like your come on my face mmmmm xxxxx

~ Regina xx

Subject: Wake up! Wake up!

You've made me crazy horny again, Ryan, all those hot hot emails xx

Xx I want to fuck you xx I want to fuck you even more now. Oh do wake up, Ryan, wake up . . .

Wake up, wake up. . .

~ Regina

14.

The box of chocolates

. . .

Marilyn's story

He asked me, "Who sent you the box of chocolates?" I told him that people who like me give me things I like. So he ate the chocolates the football player had sent me . . .

The football player who wanted to meet me had texted and said he was coming back to the city. Then he sent me a dozen pink roses and a box of chocolate truffles. He wasn't the one who took me to dinner that night, though. Instead, I had dinner with the tall sexy guy who had given me a foot massage late one night after I'd been dancing for hours.

I think I had two sangrias -- I got really tipsy. I thought it was time for him to leave because he was supposed to go to watch a basketball game at 11 and I was going to a restaurant to meet some of my friends. On the way home, I told him he should drop me off at the restaurant because I didn't want to go home, but he said why don't you go home and rest. I asked why are you telling me this, I don't see a ring on my finger. I made sure he saw me looking at my finger, to make the point.

I thought he was going to drop me off where I wanted to go. He drove to my place, so I thought I was going to take my car and leave, but he parked in the visitors parking lot and said he needed to change. By that time, I knew he was jealous and didn't want me to meet my friends -- and of course, he was also horny.

Well, I was kind of upset having him change my plans to be with my friends, but I thought, whatever, I shouldn't be drinking and driving anyway. So we went upstairs and he changed into some spare clothes he had in his trunk, while I went into my kitchen and made myself another drink.

He walked into the kitchen and began talking very seriously about us having a friends with benefits relationship and I said one of us will get hurt. He asked do you want us to stop this?

I said you started this -- you waited in the parking lot that night for me to answer the phone. He said I just wanted to taste you, you taste so good. And as he said that, he was taking off my shoes and rubbing my feet.

He asked me, who sent you the roses and chocolate? I told him that people who like me give me things I like. He said I'd like some chocolate and I said have some.

After he ate the chocolates the football player had given me, he turned around and told me to get on his back -- I was sitting on the kitchen counter. He carried me like a backpack up to my bedroom and started taking my clothes off and went down on me. He licked me until I came and then we started fucking. He said he was about to explode. I was hoping that he wouldn't come so hard that he would break the condom.

After we finished fucking, he went into the bathroom and asked me where the towels were. I said you know where the towels are and I went to sleep -- I meant it like you aren't that special anymore, so you can get your own towel. When he finished his shower, he came in and gave me a good night kiss and then he left.

15.

The building has been struck by lightning

. . .
Regina's story

"I'm leaving early and my tongue wants to lick you. . ."

"I'm wearing my suit. . . I can't come in my suit"

"Mmm hmmm, I told you I'd get you back."

Subject: No A/C in the bldg, I am leaving early ...

Ryan,

   It is stifling hot in office, over 90 degrees, and there is no air conditioning or any air circulating at all - the building was struck by lightning this afternoon and the HVAC was zapped. I am leaving -- it's nearly the end of the day, anyway, we have been sent home because of the heat -- and would love to lick you xx given the opportunity - I am not that far from home xx

~ xx Regina

Subject: Re: No A/C in the bldg, I am leaving ...

Have 2 b at meeting in 45 minutes x

Ryan

Subject: Re: No A/C in the bldg, I am leaving ...

   It takes 15 - 20 minutes for me to get home xx

Is that enough time or . . . Later, then?

~ xx Regina xx

Subject: **RE: No A/C in the bldg, I am leaving ...**

U would have to call me and I have to go at 5 xxx yur decision xxx Ryan

Subject: **Re: No A/C in the bldg, I am leaving ...**

Send me your number, I'm on my way xx

~ Regina xx

Subject: **RE: No A/C in the bldg, I am leaving ...**

Here it is, call me ... Xx Ryan

~ *In the car*

Regina drove through the traffic, expertly weaving around whatever she could, but traffic was much heavier than usual and two large commercial trucks were using the small neighborhood roads as shortcuts to the highway -- illegally, she thought, irritatedly. She tried to dial the mobile number Ryan had sent, but her phone wouldn't dial out and gave an error recording instead. She would need to add a plus in front of his phone number, since he was out of the country. She finally stopped at a light long enough to add the plus and dialed.

~ *Parked. Calling*

Regina:

Hello hot sexy man. I didn't make it home, the traffic was too heavy, so I am pulling into the parking lot at St Teresa's Catholic Church and am parking under a tree. We are going to have sneaky hot sex outside the Catholic church and scandalize all the saints. And probably end up in double hell. . .

Ryan:

I have on my suit, I cannot come on my suit that I am wearing to the meeting.

Regina:

Ah, don't worry, I'll take care of that -- I'll suck it all up. Not a drop of come will be on your suit . . . xxx

Ryan:

LOL -- now you have a four thousand mile long tongue xxx

Regina:

It's just as long as yours . . . It's always worked well before . . . xxx

Ryan:

What are you wearing? Ryan x

Regina:

I'm wearing a clingy black skirt, a tight light purple top, a black bra that makes my titties stand up high and perky -- my nipples are hard and tight and are poking against the fabric -- and I have on sheer light purple panties that you can see through to my pubic hair and my pussy. I also have on sheer black stockings and very high heels xxx Regina

Ryan:

Where are your hands? Ryan x

Regina:

One is under my skirt in my pussy, the other is actually holding the mobile, but if it weren't, my fingers would be spread between my nipples, with the heel of my hand rubbing one nipple and my fingers twisting the other one. I can actually do that while holding the mobile. My nipples are already hard and want to be rubbed against your chest.

Regina:

I want to kiss you. I want to press my lips against yours and run my tongue over your lips, then I want to put my tongue between your lips and have it touch your tongue and nibble all around your lips. Then I want to

trace my tongue around your earlobes, flicking inside
your ear, then down your neck, as I unbutton your shirt. I
want run my fingers down your chest and feel your skin
against them -- so sensuous -- I love your skin. My
mouth follows after my fingers, down your chest, sucking
in your nipples and rolling all around them, nuzzling your
midsection, and down to the waist of your trousers xxx
Regina

Ryan: (Moaning . . .)

Regina:

My my, what have you got hidden in here? I ask, as
I place my fingers inside the waist band of your trousers
and undo the clasp at the waist and put my fingers on the
zip. I want to open your zipper, but not before I kiss your
waist and your belly and lick all around the skin just
above the waist of your trousers. I take the zip in my
teeth and slowly pull it down, while looking at your
boxer shorts and burying my nose in them.

Regina:

Oh oh, what's that hard thing my nose just bumped into? The hard bit that just came alive and stood up against the cloth of your boxers and pressed through it to touch my nose? Oh, I so want to open this surprise package you put before me, so I put the fingers from both of my hands in your boxer shorts waistband and ease it down.

Regina:

Oh what a lovely lovely cock you have. Welcome to my mouth, Ryan's cock, I have somewhere warm and wet waiting for you and after you've had enough of my mouth, I have a hot wet pussy that will ease itself down on your cock and make it disappear inside, swallowing your dick inside me. Hot and wet and so wanting you, my pussy is wanting you.

Regina:

But before my pussy reunites with your cock, I want your cock in my mouth, so I can swirl my tongue all around it, and lick you until I taste the first drop of salty come at the top of your dick. Mmmm, you taste so good and I love having you in my mouth. I can't wait until I get down to your balls . . . Xxx

Ryan: (Moaning . . .)

Regina:

    Tell me what's happening with you. Is your cock stiff and standing up? Can you feel my mouth around you and my tongue licking you? Are you wanting my pussy? X

Ryan: (Moaning . . .)

Yes, I have a hard on. . .

Ryan:

I can't come on my suit. I've arrived at the building for my meeting and I am pulling into the parking lot with a hard on. The meeting is in two minutes. I just hope I can arrange this hard on so it doesn't show . . . x

Regina:

Oh, you were driving . . . Now what? You have two minutes? Can you come in two minutes? Otherwise, I'll have to suck you later to finish your tongue bath with a happy ending x.

Ryan:

I can't come in my suit before the meeting. . . I've got to go now. You just enjoy playing with yourself at St Teresa's. . . Bye . . . xoxox

Regina (out loud, but to herself):

Oh, thank you Ryan. . . Again. . . Thanks for leaving before it's over . . . That's just one more thing I'll get you back for. . . Xx

16.

The white skirt

. . .

Roxy's story

He went under my skirt, pulled my panties down, and then looked up at me from underneath my skirt and smiled. . .

He came to town to see me on
Wednesday. . .

He took the bus, so I picked him up at the
bus station. I had texted him, saying I wanted
him to come see me over the weekend and I
told him he should be sure to wear a suit,
because I wanted him to look good in front of
the girls at work. When he got off the bus, he
had on a very smart suit -- a summery, white
linen suit -- and he also wore hand-tooled deep
purple shoes just for me, because purple is my
color.

When we got back to the office, he sat in
one of the straight backed chairs and watched
me work until I was finished. I know that
chair could have not have been very
comfortable -- that was so sweet of him. After
work, I made reservations for us to have dinner
at the restaurant downtown that makes all the
food on its menu infused with chocolate.

While we were eating dinner, we were
sharing our food, eating off each other's plates
and off each others forks. He always offered
me the last bite -- I loved that. When it was
time for dessert, we chose the ones that were

made with all different kinds of chocolate -- hard, soft, caramel, white, dark, and probably something else too, I can't remember there were so many chocolates to choose from-- it was like a chocolate explosion. I kept thinking here I am with a chocolate boy in chocolate restaurant with a chocolate mojito, LOL.

After we finished, he was just . . . ummm, well, you know chocolate is an aphrodisiac, right? What I'm saying is he was already ready . . .

When we got in the car, he pulled my head towards him with both his hands on each side of my head, positioning me so he could kiss me, then he did kiss me, a deep heavy kiss, long and hard. When he finished kissing me, he said let's go home.

We drove to my apartment and got into the elevator and rode all the way upstairs to my floor without touching each other -- well, at least without touching each other as much as we wanted to. I mean, we could have done it right there in the elevator. . . that is, we could have gotten started, but not finished, I don't think . . .LOL

I opened the door and said welcome to my home. He took his overnight bag and put it into the living room, then he took my briefcase to the living room and put it right next to his bag. I closed the front door and as I did, he grabbed me, pushed me against the door, pulled my hair away, and pressed his lips into my neck and started kissing me. He got down on the floor on his knees and pulled my skirt up -- you know, I had on one of those long white A-line skirts -- and he went under my skirt and pulled it up to my waist. He kissed my bum, pulled my panties down, and then looked up at me from underneath my skirt and smiled. Then he ducked his head back under my skirt and licked me, while I was still hugging the door -- it was crazy. Somehow, he stood up so he could pull my shirt off. Now all I had on was my bra and my long white skirt. He went back down on his knees, got back under my skirt, and started licking me. While he was licking me, he was telling me how much he missed me and said that he was going to enjoy me and take his time. . .

He took me by the hand and led me into the living room, where he sat down on the chair and had me straddle him. I was going to take my bra off, but he said no, so we started kissing, deep heavy kissing. He slowly moved down my left leg to take my left shoe off, tracing my leg with his hand as he went down, then he took my other shoe off and pulled me close to him.

When he reached down into his bag to get a condom, we were kissing -- we kept on kissing as I slid his suit jacket off his shoulders and tossed it behind him, so it landed across the back of a chair. I unbuttoned his shirt and opened it up -- the whole time we never stopped kissing.

He unzipped his pants, pulled his dick out, and put the condom on. Then I sat on his dick -- his dick is really big -- while he was rocking me back and forth, pulling me closer, and holding me really tight. I could feel his dick hard against me, as he slowly took off my bra -- first the left shoulder and then the right shoulder, all while he was still kissing me. He made me stand up, so I turned around and pulled my skirt up to let him have a look, wiggling my hips from side to side, so he could get a good look at my coochie.

He asked me to show him where my bedroom was, then he walked me to the bedroom. I was about to take my skirt off, but he said no leave it on. He laid me down on the bed and went under my skirt to lick me and told me he loves tasting me -- um hummmm. Then he turned me around and pulled the skirt up so that it was covering my head -- it was so long, I couldn't see what he was doing.

He kissed my ass hole, then he started fucking me from the back. He pushed me into the mattress so my butt was sticking up higher than the rest of me, then he pushed me back down, while he was stroking inside me, slowly and deeply. He was hitting my G spot, which made me get louder with each stroke. All the while he was saying, you like that, do you like that, you like that, I know you like that, in his deep, sexy voice that turned me on so much, it made me come.

After I came, he turned me around and put his mouth in my coochie, tasting my come -- I was thinking OMG, this is a crazy motherfucker. He pulled me to the edge of the bed, lifted my legs so they were wrapped around his neck, and started fucking me again, holding up my legs and pushing my thighs down, while he stroked deeper and deeper. Then he grabbed my hands and told me to hold my legs for him, because he wanted to use his hands for something else.

He started caressing my breasts while I was holding my ankles, then he went down on on me and spread my butt cheeks and my coochie wide and licked me again. Then he started fucking me again and pushed my ankles to the side, so he could see my pretty face, he said. He started kissing me, kissing my whole body and telling me he was going to take his time and enjoy every second.

I pulled him in close to me and wrapped my legs around him so he couldn't go anywhere and I wrapped my hands around his neck so I could move him to where I wanted him to be. I told him I wanted him to come when I was coming -- I said this as I was kissing him on his ear and kissing and licking and biting him, while I was moving him so than he was stroking inside me slower and slower, long and slow.

I starting pulsing my coochie, making it tighter when he stroked in and letting it go just when he was pulling out -- I wanted to make him go crazy. He started sweating as we kept doing that -- his slow strokes in my pulsing coochie and my hands around his neck -- it really turned me on -- I was almost there.

I told him, I'm coming, come with me, daddy, I'm ready . . . as I was stroking his dick with my coochie and making him stroke me faster by pushing him down and up with my arms until we exploded together and I could feel his dick pulsing inside me. Then he pulled his dick out and licked my coochie, making me come again. He told me that I tasted so good, so good. It was so good too, but I was so sensitive after coming so many times, I had to tell him to stop.

He held me tight and I went to sleep. Later in the night, he woke me up when he stuck his dick inside me and starting fucking me again. He said he missed that, being away from me all week, he missed fucking me during the night, off and on while we were sleeping.

Do you know he is a phone sex guy too? I really love talking to him, so instead of calling my other out-of-state boyfriend who lives way down south on a sandy beach by the ocean -- I don't like that guy that much anymore -- I'm now going to call him, my new big city chocolate friend.

17.

Look! Do you like my new bra?

* * *

Regina's story

Tonight I went to the opera...then I came home and took off my clothes.

Subject: Tonight I went to the Opera...

Tonight I went to the opera . . . I have some pictures I took for you xxxooo

xxx Regina

Picture: "Leaving"
(in low cut black dress and pearls)

Picture: "Then I came home and took off my clothes . . ."
(No longer have on dress; getting undressed, only wearing lacy black bra and black bikini panties)

Picture: "Do you like my new bra?"
(Now starting to take the bra off, have one breast out, just for you . . .)

Subject: RE: Tonight I went to the Opera...

Wow!

Great pic xxx

Like the underwear xxx

Ryan

Subject: RE: Tonight I went to the Opera..

Oh, I'm glad you like them!

Take those to bed with you when you're horny xxx.

You're back in the USA?

xxx Regina

Subject: RE: Tonight I went to the Opera...

in New York x however going back tomorrow x

Ryan

Subject: RE: Tonight I went to the Opera...

Ahhh - I'll be in NYC next weekend xx you know, we could have had a really hot quickie -- you'd have to slip away from your work colleagues after I leave the play as I am running for the train. . .

We could have had hot hot sneak away from work hot sex in the hot city.

I think I need to finish the tongue bath sometime, the one I was giving you last week in the car . . .

Xxx Regina

Subject: RE: Tonight I went to the Opera...

Tell me more xx

Ryan

Subject: RE: Tonight I went to the Opera...

When you pulled into the parking lot for your meeting last Monday and I was sucking your cock...

You said: I can't come on my suit--bye.

And I said: I'll just have to finish sucking you later, which could have been our hot quickie in NYC in real time if I had gone to NYC this weekend xx LOL

~ Regina xxx

Subject: RE: Tonight I went to the Opera...

I need to switch from this phone to the computer . . .

It's easier for me to lick and fuck you on email than by this texting I'm doing now xx let me know when you want your happy ending xx

~Regina xxx

Subject: RE: Tonight I went to the Opera...

I love happy endings xxx

Ryan

Subject: RE: Tonight I went to the Opera...

Got a computer?

I will lick you xx ...

I wrote something for you some time ago about being a horny Cherokee princess and licking you like no other, mighty pale faced chief - I never sent it to you xx

~ Regina xxx

Subject: RE: Tonight I went to the Opera...

Waiting xx

Ryan

Subject: RE: Tonight I went to the Opera...

Waiting? ? ?

I just sent long text and am now in garage, going upstairs . . .

Waiting for your happy ending xxx?

Do you have email xx?

Ah -- am at computer and see an email from you . . . just a mo xx

~ Regina xxx

Subject: RE: Tonight I went to the Opera...

no mail x

Ryan

Subject: RE: Tonight I went to the Opera...

But you texted to my email address, so we're good . . .

Just a mo - I will reply to your email. . .

Did you get email on phone just now? xx

~ Regina xxx

Subject: RE: Tonight I went to the Opera...

Have PC, am in room xx

Ryan

Subject: RE: Tonight I went to the Opera...

Woo hoo xx no more texts, lots of sex . . . LOL xxx

~ Regina x

Subject: RE: Tonight I went to the Opera...

I am here xxx

Ryan

Subject: Re: Tonight I went to the Opera...

Good, Ryan, I'm horny for you xx and I have been since the night at the opera xxxx

~ Regina x

Subject: RE: Tonight I went to the Opera...

I am looking at your breasts xx

Ryan

Subject: Re: Tonight I went to the Opera...

I took a picture in the opera house during intermission (I was in a box seat) thoroughly scandalizing the man sitting in the back.

He just looked down at the floor.

I made sure I showed lots of cleavage for the photo.

My dress was very low cut, so I wore a lacy black bra, which you can see peeking out the top of my cleavage under the dress in the first picture -- unfortunately, it was too dark in the opera for the pic -- it didn't work out.

So I was at this opera with a famous tenor singing, while I was hot and wet for you and wished we could fuck behind the curtains xx then I wished we could fuck on the balcony overlooking the river, then I got home and decided I wanted to fuck you wearing my black pearls xxxx

~ Regina x

Subject: Fwd: Tonight I went to the Opera...

     So, I thought, you would probably be asleep late Saturday night when I sent the pictures, but maybe we could have hot oily Sunday morning sex when you woke up and got horny looking at my black underwear, hot oily sex in the early morning, with lots and lots of heat xxxx

~ Regina x

Subject: RE: Tonight I went to the Opera...

I love oily sex with you xxx

Ryan

Subject: RE: Tonight I went to the Opera...

Would you fuck me with your pearls xx

Ryan

Subject: Re: Tonight I went to the Opera...

With them? String of pearls? You'd have to show me how... xxxx

Regina

Subject: RE: Tonight I went to the Opera...

I could fuck you with pearls also xxx

Ryan

Subject: Fwd: Tonight I went to the Opera...

If you meant string of pearls, I only read about that in passing once, never any description of how it is pulled off, so to speak . . . had to use my imagination. . .xxxx

~ Regina x

Subject: Fwd: Tonight I went to the Opera...

Still, I'm a quick study.

I have lots of pearl necklaces. . . tell me more xx

Something about pulling the string out while coming xx is that right?

xx Regina

Subject: **RE: Tonight I went to the Opera...**

You can wrap them around my cock and I insert myself slowly - you will scream with delight xxx

Ryan

Subject: **RE: Tonight I went to the Opera...**

As you come, I take my cock out xxx

Ryan

Subject: **Re: Tonight I went to the Opera...**

I like that.

That sounds great.

Pearly cock.

I had heard it was anal. Xxx

~ Regina x

Subject: RE: Tonight I went to the Opera...

Could be anal however never tried that xxx

Ryan

Subject: Re: Tonight I went to the Opera...

What I remember is that it is called String of Pearls or Knotted Handkerchief and the string of pearls or handkerchief is inserted up your rectum, with just a bit left out to pull on -- during vaginal sex -- or whatever kind of sex we are having -- it is pulled out just as you are starting to come. . .

I think we should try the pearly cock sex and maybe the other one too -- that's your call, since it would be you with the pearls up your bum. . . xx

~ Regina x

Subject: RE: Tonight I went to the Opera...

xxx I would like you to come tonight xxx

Ryan

Subject: Re: Tonight I went to the Opera...

Oh yes, of course I'd like that ...

I came with you (imaginary you) a lot Saturday.

A lot.

I mean a lot.

Broke some record, I think.

So make me even hotter for you than I already am . .

Subject: RE: Tonight I went to the Opera...

I would like to suck you and bite your nipples xx

Show me another photo xx

Ryan

Subject: Re: Tonight I went to the Opera...

Okay.

I've got another one with another pretty bra and turquoise panties, which I took the day before I went to the opera.

Xxx Regina x

Subject: Re: Tonight I went to the Opera...

I like the pearly cock sex you told me about, Ryan.

I'm hot just thinking about it mmmmmm xxx.

I'm looking for the other bra picture now . . .

~ Regina x

Subject: RE: Tonight I went to the Opera...

Do you like anal sex xx

Ryan

Subject: Re: Tonight I went to the Opera...

Hmmm. . .

Yes and no.

I like it very much sometimes when I am very very hot and the sex is really intense and last a long time. xx

Usually though, it hurts too much, so I don't do it.

Do you?

Xxx Regina

Subject: RE: Tonight I went to the Opera...

I want to suck your nipples, I have your photo in front of me xx

Ryan

Subject: **Another pretty bra, pictures taken earlier**

Here you go -- xx

~ Regina x

Picture: *"Look - a new bra."*
(Picture of a see through lacy bra with little embroidered turquoise and purple flowers)

Picture: *"Do you like my turquoise panties?"*
(Picture of matching turquoise panties, slightly pulled down, teasing . . .)

Subject: **RE: Another pretty bra, pictures taken earlier**

I want to fuck you xxxx

Show me more pictures xx

Ryan

Subject:How about what's underneath? Picture

Here's another picture . . .

I want to fuck you too xx

Picture: *"How about what's underneath?"*
(Picture of turquoise panties pulled all the
way back with pussy lips peeking through . . .)

Subject: RE: Tonight I went to the Opera...

What were you doing on Saturday night while thinking of me xx

Ryan

Subject: Re: Tonight I went to the Opera...

Sitting in a opera box next to a lady I just met who was talking to me about the opera, never mind I had something else (hot sex with you) on my mind xx

She had the same color hair as you and gave me her business card like you did when we first met -- she told me to call her, but otherwise, there was no resemblance to you at all, LOL. . .

Xx Regina xxx

Subject: RE: Tonight I went to the Opera...

And when you got home xx

Ryan

Subject: Re: Tonight I went to the Opera...

When I got home, Ryan, I knew I wanted to undress for you, while doing a sexy classy striptease. . .

So I took the photos of me taking off the black bra xx

I wish could have taken more photos. . .

xxxx Regina

Subject: HOT

I am hot for you

xxxx Regina

Subject: **RE: How about what's underneath?**

Would you like me to lick you x

Ryan

Subject: **Re: How about what's underneath?**

Yes yes yes . . .

I love your long tongue xx

I love how it makes my clit hot mm

I love how you stick your tongue in my cunt after licking my pussy lips xx

I love how you lick around my hole and then dip your tongue in it mmmmm. . .

xxxx Regina

Subject: **RE: Tonight I went to the Opera...**

And now what are you doing now xx

Ryan

Subject: **Re: Tonight I went to the Opera...**

I have undone my bra so I can pinch my nipples xx

I have slipped down my trousers and panties xx and I am ready to moan while your tongue drives me wild xx xx

~ Regina xxx

~ *Phone call (ring-g-g)*

Ryan: What did you do in the afternoon before the opera when you were thinking of me xx? What made you come xx so much?

Regina: Ah, you always kept asking me if I had a vibrator, so I got one. . .

Regina: I named the vibrator after you, xx ha ha.

Regina: I named it Ryan LOL ~xx

Ryan: Ha ha ha xx I'm licking you now. I love your cunt. Put your hand in your pussy and move it like it is my tongue is licking you xx

Regina: Mmmmm . . .What do I taste like? xxx

Ryan: You taste like lychee fruit . . .

Regina: I love it when you suck me and lick my pussy.

Regina: I love it when you suck my clit then flick it with your tongue.

Regina: I'm going to suck you now xxx

Ryan: Oh yes. . . So good. . . Lick my horn xx

Regina: You taste really good - I love it when you come in my mouth.

Regina: I love sucking you.

Regina: I love the way your dick feels when I slide my tongue up it and back down again.

Regina: I am flicking your balls with my tongue now.

Regina: Do you like that? xxx

Ryan: Do you like my balls?

Ryan: Do you like licking them too?

Regina: I love your balls. I love licking your balls. I'm going to lick your balls and take them in my mouth xxx

Ryan: Ahhh... (Moaning)

Regina: Now I'm going to lick all around your balls and under them xxx

Ryan: Yes, yes (more moaning)

Regina: Now I'm going to turn you over and lick and nibble your bum cheeks then lick up your crack and then I am going to run my tongue around your anus.

Regina: Then I'm going to run my tongue back up to your balls and up your shaft and up to the tip of your dick and suck the bead of come that is starting to show on the end of your dick.

Regina: You're getting close.

Regina: You're going to come, I know it, you're going to come in my mouth. . .

Regina: And I am going to come too, as you come in my mouth. . .

Regina: Put your hand on my pussy, put your thumb on my clit, put your fingers in my cunt ... xxx

Ryan: I want to fuck you.

Ryan: I want to come in your cunt.

Ryan: I want to feel your cunt when I come xx. . .

Regina: Fuck me, fuck me, give me your cock. Make me come. Feel me come. . . xx

Ryan: (Heavy rapid moaning. . . then silence)

Regina: Oh, oh, oh, feel me come, I can feel it. . . I can feel it . . . Oh. . . So good. . . . xx

~ After a few moments of silence

Regina: Tell me. . . What's going on with you? Have you come? xxx

Ryan: Yes, oh yes. . . I actually came before you did xx

Regina: Mmmmm...You should tell me when you come xx.

Regina: It makes me hot xx when you come.

Regina: I can imagine your hot come spurting xx inside my cunt, thicker than my pussy juices, mixing in with them and then I can imagine I feel your cock inside me, lying down and resting, while I start to come . . . xxx

Ryan: Umm hummmmmm . . . (sighing)

Ryan: Well, Babe, I think I should take a shower now xx. I'm off xoxox

Regina: Yeah, I need one too.

Regina: I have pussy juices all over my left hand up past my wrist.

Regina: I'm saving that pussy pic I took that didn't get sent to you for later xx

Regina: Going to shower now x and thinking pearly thoughts about you xx

Ryan: Sweet dreams, Babe x

18.

In Boston on Sunday

. . .

Sara's story

If you come see me, we could have pervy sex . . .

~ *In the afternoon (via text)*

Sara: In Manhattan today, sent email xx

Sara: I heard about some pervy fun thing from my girlfriends that I think we should try. Just you wait. In the meantime, I'm thinking pearly thoughts about you xx string of pearls, pearly thoughts xx

~ *Later, around midnight . . .*

Shawn: U there x. . .

Shawn: . . . Ok maybe not. . .

Shawn: . . .R u there x. . .

Shawn: In Boston on Sunday x

~ *Two AM that morning*

Sara: Yes, back late, wee hours, I know.

Sara: I was designated driver, had to drive people home after NYC trip.

Sara: Mmm... we have some unfinished pearly business...

~ *A few minutes of resounding silence later*

Sara: Where are you?

Sara: Wake up, wake up.

Sara: I want to fuck you xx

Sara: I want to suck you (mmm...).

Sara: I want you to lick me xx --

Sara: I want feel your tongue licking my cunt. . .

Sara: I want you to make me come.

Sara: I want you to come in my mouth . . .

Sara: The last thing I remember, we were having a very nice hot conversation about some mildly pervy sex . . .

Sara: You know, it's only 60 minutes by train to Boston. . .

Sara: Whenever you're that close, you could always invite me up for, uh, "dinner."

Sara: I mean, just saying . . . xx

~ *Six AM that morning*

Shawn: Well you are welcome to come to see me x

Shawn: We could have pervy sex x

Shawn: At airport be there at 1x

~ *Seven AM that morning*

Sara: Just woke up

Sara: Will you pick me up at the train station?

Shawn: Don't have car

Shawn: Am staying at airport hotel x

Sara: Okay, need to check transport between train station & airport

Shawn: Staying at hotel on airport boulevard

Sara: How long do we have, meaning when should I book return ticket

Shawn: Book return for late evening x

Sara: Okay give me a few moments ...

Sara: So you arrive at airport at 1, hotel 1:30 to 2?

Shawn: Hotel 5 mins from airport so should b there at 1:30 x

Sara: Return trains at 9, 10, or 11PM, no need for early check in. Which?

Shawn: Flight leaving so may not get texts until 9ish.

Sara: Need to know when to leave you . . .

Shawn: Whatever u want

Shawn: U decide xx

Sara: x This cd b fun

Shawn: I am sure it will b

Sara: Okay have train ticket, arrive station at 12:30

Sara: Dunno ground transportation yet, cd be at hotel b4 you, look in lobby for hot black dress, will txt

Sara: Rtn train 11:30PM

Sara: Off 2 shower

Sara: Are you flying on American? Which flight ?

Shawn: Yes, American, depart 1102

~ *A few hours later*

Sara: On train, boarding...

Sara: Shuttle between train station & hotel stops at airport.

Sara: Will pretend not to know you if we share transport to hotel. LOL

Shawn: That works LOL x

~ *An hour later*

Shawn: Landed

Sara: x On shuttle train to airport ETA 10 mins approx

Shawn: Have to work on computer for half an hour x

Sara: xx Working at hotel on computer?

Sara: Am almost at your terminal

Sara: R u using computer at airport lounge or at hotel?

Shawn: Yes, will use computer in room, need WiFi for connectivity

Sara: Where are you right now?

Sara: I am in the baggage claim area for your flight and don't see you anywhere.

Sara: Let me know where you are.

Sara: I'm feeling lost - I hate that.

Shawn: Get on shuttle for hotel beside baggage claim

Shawn: Just missed you, was on shuttle

Sara: Bugger! Will be on the next one xx

Sara: Pls text your room number as soon as you get it. Promise to quit being so lost & anxious & needy LOL xx

Sara: On shuttle. On way to hotel now xx

Shawn: Ok

~ *At the hotel*

When Sara walked into the hotel, she saw Shawn at hotel reception, waiting to check in. She leaned sultrily against the wall of the hotel, parallel to him, about 30 feet away, and looked at him, willing him to look up at her and see her in her short, tight, black dress as he was texting her:

Shawn: No room yet--2 early

He looked up from his phone as he sent the text, saw her out of the corner of his eye, and he smiled a wicked, sly smile. He and Sara walked over separately to the lobby with chairs and couches, where other people were also waiting for rooms to become available. Shawn started to sit down on the couch, then decided to sit at one of the cafe tables and looked at her, signaling her with his eyes to follow him. Sara walked up to the cafe table and asked him if he minded if she joined him. He said, don't mind if you do, madam. So she sat down and began to read a book on her notebook computer, while he set up his laptop, notebook, and cellphone to work for a while. They sat inches apart, pretending they didn't know each other, the heat between them burning hot. . .

Shawn: Sent you an email -- my phone is dying, so using email

Shawn: . . .Reply to email x

Sara: Your email has been sorted to a folder on my laptop @ home, which I forgot to turn off in my rush to leave this morning, so I barely saw your email just now ...

Sara: Sigh...

Sara: Texts work, though.

Sara: Your email said something about what one of us would do to the other?

Sara: I have on a sexy black bra ... Xx

Sara: I brought almond oil . . . Xx . . . mmmm

Shawn: Good I could do with massage

Shawn: What would you like me to do to you x

Sara: I want to be licked

Sara: I want you to kiss me while pinching my nipples ...

Sara: I want you to run your hands down my back to my bum and feel your nails on my skin

Sara: I want you to bite my neck and my nipples

Sara: I want you to make my cunt sopping wet

Sara: I brought something else too. . .

Sara: A surprise, but not a big surprise.

Sara: And here -- I'll text you a nice, sexy naked picture of me, to keep you company until the room is available.

Shawn: I have a hard on x

Sara: Mmmmm I want it in my mouth xx

Shawn: What else? What else would you like me to do?

Sara: Wd u like to take off my bra?

Sara: Wd u like to put your mouth on my nipples?

Sara: Wd u like to suck my nipples?

Sara: Wd u like to roll your tongue around them?

Sara: Wd u like to nibble them?

Sara: Wd u like to bite them as you slip your cock inside my pussy?

"I have a room," Shawn said, walking by her.

"Did you text me the number?" she asked.

Shawn smiled archly and pointed to the room key card he had slipped under the stand that held her computer notebook.

"Who's going up first, you or me," she asked

"I'll go," he said, "give me a few minutes."

...   .

She stayed in the lobby at the table and read a little longer, then went to the restroom in the lobby. She rinsed her pussy with wet paper towels, since she had been traveling a few hours since her morning shower and she wanted to be clean when he licked her. Then Sara rode up the elevator, walked down the long hallway, and opened the hotel room door.

Shawn walked out of the shower, with a white towel wrapped around him, put his hands on both sides of her head, holding her as he kissed her, heavy and deeply, his tongue against hers. As he did, he reached down to the hem of her short black dress, lifted it up over her head and threw it aside. Then he slid down the straps of her black lace bra and stopped kissing her for a moment to smile as her breasts popped out of the bra cups. Still smiling, a wicked smile now, he grabbed her nipples and began to twist and pinch them between his fingers. Sometimes it hurt and she said OUCH, but he didn't stop. She had thrown her bra over by the dress and had eased her panties and stockings down her thighs, so they would graze his dick and balls -- he hadn't entered her, but she could feel his cock, stiff between her pussy and her stockings. He stood back, still smiling, and kept on pinching her nipples, as she came over and over again. She pressed her wet cunt against his thigh, pulsing against his leg each time she came. She almost fell several times, but he held her upright when her knees buckled. He pulled her against him, one of his hands working her nipples. He wrapped his other hand in her hair at the nape of her neck, and pulled it, so that her face looked up at his face, while his forearm pushed her against him, and continued to hold her up.

"Oh god," she said, as she was coming the third time, "Oh god, Shawn, oh god."

When she felt the final pulsing wave, Shawn dropped back on the bed, lying face up diagonally across the bed, and looked up at her as he said, "Suck me. Suck me. I want you to suck me."

Sara climbed on the bed, kneeling over his cock and licked it around the head before taking it into her mouth. She pressed her thighs against his, so that her stockings touched the tender part of his buttocks and his balls and her nipples touched his thighs. He began to stroke inside her mouth, much faster than he usually did and even deeper, so that his cock went deep into her throat and made her gasp. He continued stroking, even more intensely, so much so that she was surprised to find she was crying with each stroke. She realized that she would soon come again -- and she did, just as Shawn's come exploded into her mouth and as he shouted loudly, "oh my god, Sara, oh my god," she came, her cunt shuddering against his thigh.

Shawn pulled back the covers and got under them and Sara moved so that she was lying beside him. "I want my skin touching yours," she said. She reached for the bottles of the almond massage oil and the sandalwood oil she had brought to scent it, rubbed a few drops on her fingers, and held it to his nose, "Smell this. It's for your massage, later."

"Ummm," Shawn smiled, as his arms encircled her, pulled her close to his chest, and they fell slept.

. . .   .

He opened his eyes, turned to look at her, and asked, "What time is it? Did I go to sleep?"

"Yes, for a couple of hours," she said. "I slept for a little while, then I lay here against you and watched you breathing in and out. Now roll over and face downwards, so I can work my magic."

She reached under the covers and found the almond and the sandalwood oil bottles, then she straddled him, so that her pussy was pressed against his back. She drizzled a mixture of the two oils into her palm and started rubbing it into his neck and shoulders, then down his arms, stopping to nibble and suck his fingertips before she oiled his hands. This is hot, she thought, as she continued letting oil drops fall on his back as she kneaded his muscles until they were no longer tight. She continued down his legs to his feet, sucking his toes, then bottom of his feet before she oiled them. She noticed that the soles of his feet were much rougher than the last time they met, so she took extra time to oil his feet, to make them softer. While she was massaging him, Sara made sure she brushed her pussy in the oil on his back and began to massage him, laying her whole body on top of his.

All during the massage, Shawn lay face downwards and didn't make a sound -- no feedback at all to tell her what was nice, no moans of pleasure, nothing -- but she was used to this.

Suddenly, he came alive, rose up from the covers, turned over, and pushed her down where he had lain, so that he was kneeling over her, his cock hard and his sly, wicked smile wide on his face. He grabbed her by her thighs, pulled her cunt up next to his crotch, then took his cock and lay it on top of her pussy, so that the tip of his cock was touching her clit as he looked into her eyes. Oh, Sara thought, this is so hot, and she began to shiver in anticipation. Shawn picked up her hand, placed it on her cunt, and rubbed her hand against her clit and his cock. Then he moved his dick so that the tip was against her wet pussy lips.

"Slide in," she said, "slide inside me. . . You are so sexy. . . sexy man"

. . .   .

Afterwards, they lay in each others arms again, until Shawn got out of bed, went to the bathroom and drew a deep, hot bath. "I love a bath," he said. A slight scent of massage oil wafted in the air as he stepped into the tub and lay back for several minutes with his eyes closed.

"Don't let the water out," Sara said as he started to drain the bath. "I want a bath too."

"Oh," he said, turning on the hot tap and refilling the bath for her. "I thought you were ready."

"Ready? She said, "Look at me. Do I look ready?" Sara stretched out her arms as she stood naked before him as he lay in the bath. "I suppose I could be ready for something, but not for walking out the door. Besides, you haven't smacked my butt yet."

"You didn't ask me to," Shawn laughed, as he got out of the tub.

"You know I always want you to smack my butt, anytime," she smiled, as she slipped into the hot bath and closed her eyes.

"How about dinner before you go," he asked, when she had finished with the bath, toweled off, and was dressing.

. . .   .

They took a taxi into town. As he was talking to the driver, she reached into her satchel and pulled out the strand of pearls she'd brought. She looked knowingly at him and he smiled slyly back at her -- the pearly sex would have to wait for another time . . .

Shawn took her to a restaurant downtown -- old style Cuban, with an open patio trimmed with lots of decorative wrought iron and tall, pale yellow stucco walls with vines growing down the walls to the terra cotta tiled floors. He ordered wine. They were seated side by side on the balcony outside, so it was easier for them to eat from each others plates while they talked.

After dinner, he hailed a cab and took her to the train station. He got out of the cab when it stopped, opened the door for her, hugged her and said, as he always did when they parted, "I'll see you when I see you . . ."

Sara looked into his eyes, but said nothing, in case it showed in her voice how hard it was for her to leave him. Instead, she picked up his hand and placed his fingers on her heart for a few beats, then walked inside the terminal without looking back as the cab pulled away.

~ *Later that night (via text)*

Shawn: Goodnight xx

Sara: x I caught 9.30 train because it was running late, I'm almost back home now. . .

Sara: You are very sexy xx after being massaged.

Shawn: Mmm . . .Have sweet dreams xx

19.

The little red dress

. . .

Mariah's story

So his brother went over to the booth and took the red dress off the hanger and made me put it on.

So he bought me this red dress. You didn't see the red dress? I've got it hanging up on the hook on the wall in the back room. . . You've got to see it, it's really, really hot.

On Sunday, first he texted me, then he called me. He wanted me to come over to his hotel and have dinner with him again, but I really didn't have time, so I went over late, around 10:30 or 11. He lit up, like he always does when he first sees me, and he smiled really warmly and said hi, how are you, I've missed you so much.

We were in the executive lounge on the 8th floor and we were on the balcony, smoking cigars. There was some kind of something going on in the lounge, like some charity event with rich older ladies looking around, shopping. You know they spend ten grand a year, those ladies? There was a little booth set up to sell things for fund raising for the charity and that's where the ladies were looking around, that little booth.

That's when he saw this red dress. His brother was there too and his brother asked what is your size and I said size 6. So his brother went over to the booth and took the red dress off the hanger and made me put it on. It cost around $300 and it was hot, really hot. It was so hot that all the rich older ladies turned around and looked at me when I put it on.

He looked at me, first deep in my eyes and then slowly, all up and down my body, taking it all in, me in that red dress. He said you're so beautiful, you're so stunning, while he was hugging me and holding my hips and I thought -- in front of everyone! His brother said, yeah I'm going to buy this for my brother's wife. I was trying to hide my left hand -- I thought I need to ask him to buy me a ring, this little red dress is going to get me in trouble.

So we were on the penthouse making out and he was getting aroused and his brother brought me a glass of riesling and sat down next to him. He just pulled me closer and I felt his hands were like, um, sweaty. I knew that he would really want to have me tonight, in the red dress. I thought I just can't do it, I just can't cross that line . . then one of his cousins came up and started talking business. The business talk turned me on -- they were talking about office space and purchasing a commercial property and one of them said it was only $750K -- I want that property. That's in cash -- it's a foreclosure and I'm thinking that's a lot of money that he has, to casually toss around stuff about buying a building for three quarters of a mill.

Twenty or thirty minutes later, he had drunk some more and was really wasted. I decided I needed to go home because I was really tired. He walked me to the elevator. All the time, he was kissing me and pulling me closer to his body and grabbing my butt in the elevator and stroking me up and down my thighs and my butt with his hands all over me. I was thinking OMG, they don't have cameras in this elevator, do they? He was grabbing my waist and grabbing my hair and pulling me closer, right up to him, face to face, body to body -- you've really got to see that red dress, I mean really -- it's hot. So we were making out as the elevator went down the eight floors and just before the elevators doors opened, we pushed the button to close the doors again and kept on making out, hot and heavy.

Then the doors opened and we were in the lobby. He walked me to the car and he told me again that he really missed me. I sat in my car and before he closed the door, he reached in his pocket and slid a few hundred bucks in the car and I smiled goodbye and I drove home.

So, on to the next one. . .

20.

Not if I see you first

. . .

Sara's Story

"Do you have a webcam? I want to fuck you with your vibrator and watch you come. You could get on Skype and I could watch . . ."

Subject: **Not if I see you first ...**

Shawn,

I hope you are well xx

Here's something for you xx

Picture: *(Sara running naked up staircase, looking backwards over her shoulder)*

~ Sara

Subject: **RE: Not if I see you first ...**

I am thank you - nice photo xx

Shawn

Subject: **Random thoughts**

I am at a meeting right now, sitting around a long u-shaped table, imaging you under the table with your hands parting my thighs and your head between my legs and your mouth against my panties, moving them aside, so you can touch your tongue to my clit. xx

~ Sara

~ *Later that night*

Subject: RE: Random thoughts

Love your thoughts x

Shawn

Subject: Re: Random thoughts

    xx

~ Sara xoxoxo

Subject: RE: Random thoughts

I hope you are well xx

Shawn

Subject: Re: Random thoughts

I am, thanks.

Still, I could feel even better xx

~ Sara

Subject: RE: Random thoughts

What do you mean xx

Shawn

Subject: Re: Random thoughts

I was just thinking how much I love sucking you... Xx

~ Sara

Subject: RE: Random thoughts

That is a nice thought x

Shawn

Subject: Re: Random thoughts

Ahhhh ...

You twisted my nipples and made me come at least three times before I barely got though the hotel door xx

You are so sexy xx

I loved the deep throat thing you did when I was sucking you xx - it was so intense, it made me cry xx

And then, after I massaged you, you knelt before me and pulled me up to your thighs xx and laid the tip of your cock right up next to my clit-- I still get shivers over that xx

~ Xxx Sara

Subject: RE: Random thoughts

Ahhh now I have a hard on xx

Shawn

Subject: Re: Random thoughts

I want to fuck you xx

Are you horny?

I could make you horny xx

~ Sara xxx

Subject: RE: Random thoughts

Make me horny x

Shawn

Subject: Re: Random thoughts

Ah, see what I mean...

I want to fuck you xx

Let's have fun with your stiff cock xx

~ Sara xxx

Subject: RE: Random thoughts

LOL xxx let's have fun x

Shawn

Subject: Re: Random thoughts

I want to lick you xx

I want to run my tongue up your thighs and around your belly and then up your cock, while my breasts are pressed against your balls xx

~ Sara xxx

Subject: Re: Random thoughts

I want to roll my tongue around the head of your cock xx . . .

I want you to cup your hands around my bum while I am licking you xx

~ Xxx Sara x

Subject: RE: Random thoughts

That sounds lovely x

Shawn

Subject: Re: Random thoughts

I want you to run your nails lightly up my bum and up my back, then down again and stroke my bum while I start to take you in my mouth xx

~ Sara xxx

Subject: RE: Random thoughts

Sounds wonderful x

Shawn

Subject: Re: Random thoughts

I want you to push your cock into my mouth as I suck you xx and I want to hold your cock with my lips and stroke your shaft with my tongue xx

~ Sara xxx

Subject: RE: Random thoughts

Yum x

Sounds wonderful x

Shawn

Subject: Re: Random thoughts

I want you to know how turned on I am when I am sucking you xx

I want you to feel my wet cunt against your thigh and I want you to grab my hair at the nape of my neck while I am sucking you and hold my head as you push your cock in my mouth and pull it out xx

~ Xx Sara xx

Subject: RE: Random thoughts

Yummy xx

Do you like that? X

Shawn

Subject: Re: Random thoughts

Oh yes, I love it when you pull my hair at the back of my head and hold my head with both your hands.

I want you to move my head as you move in my mouth.

I want to rub my nipples against the top of your thighs, right where your lush pubic hair starts and I will get even wetter, my cunt against your thighs, as my nipples touch your pubic hair xx

~ Sara xx xx xx

Subject: RE: Random thoughts

You are very horny? X

Shawn

Subject: Re: Random thoughts

Oh my god, oh yes I am so horny for you.

All day today, I've seen your cock stiff and knew it wanted to be in my mouth and my mouth wanted your cock inside -- all day and even more days than just today xx

I am so horny for you.

And I am wet right now.

And I want you xx

~ Sara xxx

Subject: RE: Random thoughts

I want to see you playing xx . . .

But I am in a bedroom next to my relatives who are visiting this week x

Shawn

Subject: **Re: Random thoughts**

Ah well, you will have to see me in your imagination then xx because I am very hot for you xx very, very hot xx . . .

I want to feel your lovely smooth skin and trace the line that separates your golden tan from the untanned part on your bum. I want to trace around the cheeks of your bum, first with my fingers and then with my tongue. Xx

~ Sara xxx

Subject: **Re: Random thoughts**

I want to hear you moan as you are stroking in my mouth and I want you to know I am moaning too, but my moans are muffled because your cock is filling up my mouth and my mouth is so wet and your cock is so hard xx

~ Sara xxxx

Subject: RE: Random thoughts

Are you playing xx?

Shawn

Subject: Re: Random thoughts

Yes xx my fingers are on my nipples.

I'm wishing your fingers were there instead.

I am wanting you xx

I am hot for you xx

I am wet for you xx

And I am imagining you lying on the bed face downwards as I am naked, rubbing oil on you and kneading your back

xx Sara xx

Subject: RE: Random thoughts

Have you Skype?

Shawn

Subject: Re: Random thoughts

Yes, but I don't know how to start it -- I never have used it

xx Sara

Subject: RE: Random thoughts

Well you could get on Skype and I could watch you come xx

Shawn

Subject: Re: Random thoughts

Ah, just a mo. . .

I have something I meant to send you xx

A surprise xx

It will come to you by phone xx

~ Sara

Subject: Red hot summer 1

> **Pictures:** *(One dozen) Sara in a red dress, stripping down to a lacy red bra and sheer lacy red panties before slowly taking them off)*

Subject: RE: Red hot summer 3

Wow! horny red !! X

Shawn

Subject: Red hot summer 4

Have you Skype loaded xx?

Shawn

Subject: RE: Red hot summer 4

Yes -- sounds like fun xx a few more red hot pics to go xx

~ Sara xxx

Subject: RE: Red hot summer 5

Fantasia xx

Shawn

Subject: RE: Red hot summer 6 (I think, losing count)

Is this live? X

Shawn

Subject: RE: Red hot summer 8

Now you need to go on Skype x

Shawn

Subject: Re: Red hot summer 8

Okay, just a mo xx.

Do you like my red hot striptease? Xx

~ Sara xxx

Subject: RE: Red hot summer 11

Yes, I do.

You are making me very horny tonight x

Shawn

Subject: Re: Red hot summer 11

Good xx

And yes, I am very horny for you, too xx

I was horny for you earlier, but I am very, very horny for you now xx

I went to the museum of sex in NYC last Sunday xx there were lots of play toys.

I got a few . . .

Xx Sara

Subject: Re: Red hot summer 12

I'm not upstairs yet, Shawn. . .

But I am naked and I am now going to try to figure out what to do (I've forgotten my password, geez). . .

Just think of my mouth swallowing your cock xx

~ Sara xxx

Subject: RE: Red hot summer 12

Go to Skype and they will send you a new password. X

Shawn

Subject: Re: Red hot summer 12

Okay, Skype remembers me and my password.

Now what do I do?

How do I find you?

Use your email address?

Xx Sara

Subject: RE: Red hot summer 8

Use my Skype handle.

I have sent you a request, but I have no cam and can't talk xx.

I can watch you come as you play with your vibrator and with your fingers xx

Shawn

Subject: Re: Red hot summer 11

Ooooh, that sounds hot.

I must take this laptop upstairs...

The vibrators are upstairs by the bed, in the cupboard with the sexy books and massage oil xx

If you have no cam, then you can hear me, but can't see me?

Xxx Sara

Subject: RE: Red hot summer 11

I think I can see you, but you can't see me x

Shawn

Subject: Re: Red hot summer 8

I am upstairs with my laptop and have the vibrators.

I will let you know when I am on Skype

xx Sara

Subject: RE: Red hot summer 8

You there? X

Shawn

Subject: Re: Red hot summer 8

I am signed in.

Are you are ready?

Can you come where you are, in your current setting?

Or will I just make you wish you could come? LOL xx

~ Sara xxx

~ On Skype

[8/8/11 12:23:15 AM] Shawn_Douglas: You call me and see if I can see you xx

[12:24:22 AM] Shawn_Douglas: I can hear you, but cannot see you - can you try video?

[12:29:08 AM] Shawn_Douglas: Beautiful

[12:30:00 AM] Shawn_Douglas: Lost connection.

[12:30:08 AM] Shawn_Douglas: Back again.

[12:30:29 AM] Shawn_Douglas: I cannot see you.

[12:30:34 AM] Shawn_Douglas: I got you back. Beautiful.

[12:31:02 AM] Shawn_Douglas: I want to fuck you with your vibrator xx

Sara: Oh no, the screen's gone black.

Sara: Why's that?

Sara: Ah... See, this is what happens when I kick the computer power cord out of the socket while I am fucking you over the video cam . . . LOL

[12:32:05 AM] Shawn_Douglas: LOL xx

[12:32:13 AM] Shawn_Douglas: You use that vibrator a lot?

[12:32:52 AM] Shawn_Douglas: I am here. I love watching you.

[12:32:58 AM] Shawn_Douglas: I can see you, every part of you.

[12:35:22 AM] Shawn_Douglas: I'm very horny for you. I have a very big hot horn.

[12:42:06 AM] Shawn_Douglas: Wow, oh wow, you're coming. I just came too . .

[12:42:34 AM] Shawn_Douglas: Good night. Sweet dreams to you, too xx

21.

Would you like to massage me?

. . .

Stella's story

"Tell me!! Would you like to massage me?"

Would you like to massage me?? Tell me!! X Scott

Yes, I'd love to massage you, Scott - I'll need a little help at first with this, but I'm a quick study. Will you talk me through it? Get me started? I'll need:

-oil (warm? what kind do you like)

-you naked

-where? bed, cushions in front of fire? another place? xxx Stella x

I know, in front of the fire . . . Xxx Stella x

Warm oil with a nice aroma in front of the fire or on bed xx Scott

Warm oil, okay I've warmed the oil . . .xxx Stella x

You can start with my back and shoulders x Scott

Ah, you see, I told you I was a quick study.. . Where do I start? Your feet? Your head? I think your feet. .. Which? xxx Stella x

You decide - I am under your spell whilst you massage xx Scott

Okay, moving away from your feet for now . . .xxx Stella x

You are lying facing downward, with your face turned to the side. xxx Stella x

I pour the oil, almond I think, it smells like almonds, in my palm and rub it between my hands. . . I put my warm oily hands at the base of your neck . . .xxx Stella x

I am relaxing xx Scott

I touch the back of your neck with my fingertips and press them into your skin. . .

xxx Stella x

Keep going xx Scott

I move my fingertips slightly back and forth as I trace along from your neck along the top of your shoulders . ...xxx Stella x

I feel the tension in your back, but it wants to leave. . . xxx Stella x

I press my fingertips in more deeply and continue to slightly rotate my fingers xxx Stella x

I press more of my palms into your shoulders and move my hands in very small back and forth, rotating motions xxx Stella x

I am sitting beside you, but I decide to straddle your back and bend over. Xxx Stella

My nipples graze your back.xxx Stella x

My hands are on the top of your shoulders now. . .xxx S x

My hands are cupped over your shoulders now, rolling in slight movements, pressing deeply. xxx Stella x

I am up on my knees over your back, and lean back so that my pubic area is now against your buttocks.

My oily hands are moving down your upper arms . . . pressing in . . .xxx Stella x

I think I will do one arm at a time, so now both my hands are on your left upper arm and moving down to your elbow and around it. xxx Stella x

More oil now . . . Xxx Stella x

Yum, keep going -- sounds wonderful xx Scott

I lift your arm and stretch it out, then put my fingers back just above your upper elbow and pull my fingers down your sinews, down to your lower arm. xxx Stella x

I wrap my hands and my fingers around your lower arm and continue to press in, rotating slightly with my fingers, and pull your arm outwards, as I move my fingers down to your palm. xxx Stella x

I am due in a meeting in a few minutes xxx I hope I don't walk in with a hard on xx. Scott

Ok. . .Scott, you are very greedy, when it comes to pictures. . . don't think I haven't noticed. . . I might work my feelings about this into your massage, somehow, when you don't expect it (smiling archly) . . . just wait and see . . . Xxx Stella x

~ *Hiatus* . . .

I am back & will get you photo when time is permitting xxx. Scott

Scott, You're back? Do you want to finish your massage or do you have to be useful? xxx Stella x

I was useful while you were gone to your meeting: took shower (w/o you, too bad); scheduled multiple electrical repairs resulting from power outage over Holidays (all for Friday AM - don't arrive at the airport then, unless

you want to share me); started application for another position, so I can stop feeling bored at work; signed up for hot sexy dance and fitness classes downtown. . . enough useful stuff for now. . . xxx Stella x

Back to you, hot sexy Scott, mmmm . . let me know when we're resuming your massage. I left you when I was moving from your left hand to your right. . . xxxooo, Hot and horny for you, xxx Stella x

We can continue this massage later, if you like . . . I am off work today (it's a holiday), so I thought I'd spend it in bed with you . . . xxx Stella

Or, we could do your right arm . . . X Stella

This time, I'll start with your fingers and work my way back up to your shoulder . . . xxx Stella x

But first -- going to check on essential oils, upstairs. Back in a mo. xxx Stella

You're good xxx continue, please xx keep going xx Scott

I just located aromatherapy oils upstairs, good to mix for massage oils, I hear. Almond (lots), jojoba, lavender (sleep inducing, maybe not), eucalyptus, tangerine, sandalwood (my favorite) . . .xxx Stella x

Back to you . . . here is where we left it: I gently press against your palm and the back of your hand and I pull on each of your fingers, one at a time, then go back and rub my palm against yours. Xxx Stella

I lift your arm and stretch it out, then put my fingers back just above your upper elbow and pull my fingers down your sinews, down to your lower arm. I wrap my hands and my fingers around your lower arm and continue to press in, rotating slightly with my fingers, and pull your arm outwards, as I move my fingers down to your palm. xxx Stella x

I roll my palms around your fingers, pressing in, then pulling. I move over to your right hand, pick up your palm and place it over my heart, then put your hand back in my palm. . . xxx Stella x

I drizzle some more oil on my palm and rub it into your palm, between your fingers, alongside the backs and down the sides, one by one, pulling them as I press in. xxx Stella x

I press my thumbs into the joints where your fingers join your palms and roll my fingers over them. xxx Stella x

I circle my hands around your wrist, with my fingers pressed on the underside of your lower arm, and pull upwards, while pressing in. xxx Stella x

I reach your elbow and press my fingers deep into your skin just under your elbow, on your lower arm (I can smell one of the oils I just brought down from upstairs in the little wooden box with a brass hinge and lock -- I think I'm smelling sandalwood, but maybe something more aromatic. It is really adding to this scenario, nice . . .) xxx Stella x

I slide my palm over your elbow, pressing down, deeply, and am now above your elbow. I press my fingers against your sinews, which are tight, and I continue to press, until they start to yield. xxx Stella x

I continue up your upper arm, pressing my fingers into your upper arm and making little back-forth, rotating movements, until I get to your shoulder . . .xxx Stella x

I reach your right shoulder and press my fingers into your upper arm, just below the curve of your shoulder, then drag my fingers, pressing into you, hard, over the curve up on your shoulder. xxx Stella x

I take both my hands, oily again and smelling very aromatic, and press my fingers at the base of your skull, bending over you, with my nipples grazing your back. xxx Stella x

I drag my fingers, pressing in hard, the length of your spine, all the way down to your coccyx and can't resist cupping your buttocks for a moment, rounding my hands around them. . . xxx Stella x

Then, while cupping your buttocks with my oily hands, I bend over and take a sharp nip on each of your buttocks **(ow! you say)** *--* **_that's for not sending me pictures_** *. . .xxx Stella x*

LOL xxxx Scott

I then take both my hands, one on each of your buttocks, and press them in hard and push up on either side of your spine, back up to your shoulders.xxx Stella x

When I am at the top of your torso, I move both my hands to either side of your spine and press my fingers hard into your back, rotating and moving my fingers back and forth . . . xxx Stella x

*I am astride you and am leaning over you, my pubic hair
is grazing your buttocks, my nipples are touching you just
below your shoulder blades, and my hair, which is now
oily, is trying to stick to the sides of your body. I move my
breasts back and forth, so that my nipples dance a little
on your back. I make tight circle motions into your back
with my fingers cupped and pressing in hard . . xxx Stella
x*

Now I have a hard on xxx Scott

*Good, I say, and lovely it is too, but back to your
massage, until you stop me…xxx Stella x*

*On to your lower body. . . I oil my hands again and go
back to your buttocks, my hands around them. I think
about nipping you again, and smile wickedly, but
don't . . . I roll my hands over your buttocks, pressing my
fingers into your flesh, then I move below, to your upper
right thigh first. xxx Stella x*

Yum - have a hard on xx Scott

I put both hands in a circle to encircle as much of your upper thigh as I can, trying not to get distracted by your pubic hair and your hard on and your other lovely naughty bits. xxx Stella x

I press my palms against your skin, with my fingers pressed in hard too. My thumbs are on the inside of your thigh and my fingers are on the outside. I press and drag my hands down your thigh, while slightly moving my fingers back and forth. . . until I get just above your knee. xxx Stella x

Yum still have hard on - this is very horny xxx Scott

I stop at your knee and put both my hands above your knee and press my mouth against the flesh on your inside thigh while I rotate my fingers. . .xxx Stella x

It is very hard for me not to go on up with my mouth to your balls and lick behind them. . . I want you in my mouth. . . but later for that . . xxx Stella x

You are making me very very horny xx Scott

*I move below your knee, with my hands encircling your
calf. I decide to keep my mouth pressed hard against
your leg, as I move downward to your ankle.xxx Stella x*

*I reach your ankle and let my fingers roll over your heel.
I pull my fingers down over your heel, to the underside of
your foot. I knead your foot from the underneath,
starting at the heel and working up to the instep. My
mouth is very hungry for your skin. . . xxx Stella x*

xxx mmm still horny xxx Scott

*I press my mouth against your instep and I suck your
foot, my tongue is on the underside of your foot, and my
hands are kneading the upperside of your foot while I am
pressing my mouth hard against your instep. I move up
your foot to your toes and take each one, one by one, in
my oily fingers and stretch each one, while flicking my
tongue from your instep to the ball of your foot, to
between your toes. . . xxx Stella x*

I have to go to another meeting & wont be back until
late..... please continue the story so that I can read
when I get back xxx Scott

~A few moments of silence later

~ Stella: You have to . . . ??? Then you say, "Go on and continue to write about massaging me, even though I'm not there."???

-- Hmmm, I'm crossing my arms, my eyes are not quite flashing, not quite yet. . .

Sigh . . .

Maybe your masseuse needs a lunch break . . . real time sexy stories like this are much better with even the tiniest bit of interaction . . .

I'll finish your massage story after lunch, since I can't exactly put together a job application while my pussy is dripping wet from your kisses this morning and my hair and hands and body are covered in heavily aromatic massage oil. . . and my mind is deeply mesmerized with your skin, your crotch, your smell, every part of you.

So, let me know when you are back and I will send you the rest of your completed massage, not written in real time, but it will make you sizzle, nonetheless. All yours.

Just for you. Customized. Exclusive. One of a kind. . . .Xxx Stella x

~The rest of the massage

As I am massaging your toes, I nibble just a bit at the base of your toes, before putting them in my mouth and sucking hard, then I lick your toes and move over to your other foot, the left one . . .

Before I can think about it, my mouth is around your toes, licking each one of them, then nibbling down the bottom of your foot to your instep. . . I open my whole mouth and take in your instep, my tongue flicking the skin of your sole.

My fingers are rolling around your toes and my thumbs are pressed just below the ball of your foot, then move down, pressing your instep, where it joins with your heel.

I take my hand and cup it around your heel and pull it, as I go up our left ankle, pressing hard with my thumbs against your tendons and sucking your skin.

I stroke my fingers upward, up your calf, then encircle it and press my fingers, as the rotate in tight circles and move back and forth.

I'm just below your knee with my hands and grasp the meat of your thigh above your knee with my mouth and suck.

I am kneading your thighs with my hands and sucking your inner thighs with my hot mouth.

I move on up toward your upper thighs and am barely able to continue, from looking at your cock, your balls, the seam from under your balls to your anus. . .

I am having tremors in my pussy just looking at your crotch.

I want you in my mouth.

I move my head between your thighs and put my slippery, oily hands on your hips and move them to your buttocks.

I inhale the smell of you, so intoxicating.

My tongue reaches out to touch just below and underneath your balls.

I run my tongue under and around your balls. My hands are resting in the tangled curls of your pubic hair.

I slide around and you move too, so that we are upside down spoons, but I am curled up with my mouth to your genitals.

I am on the outside, and my breasts are pressed against your thighs and your crotch and feeling your pubic hair.

I trace my fingers up and down the shaft of your penis, my thumbs on the inside.

My mouth opens to take in as much of your balls as I can, my tongue is flicking around the edges and the sides and the surfaces.

I move my mouth down below your balls, onto the seam that runs to your anus.

My tongue presses hard and wet against you as I move on back to your buttocks, licking on the way.

I bury my mouth into your buttocks and suck your anus and lick around it, then over to one of your butt cheeks, the right one, and nip it, in passion this time, and lick my way over to your other butt cheek and nip you there too.

My tongue is still licking you, my breasts and your balls are dancing with each other, pinging against each other.

I run my tongue back down over your anus, up to your balls and up the shaft of your cock.

It's time you gave up that hard on -- spurt hot salty come into my mouth, I say, I want your come in my mouth, as I come. I want you. I want you. I want you. . . Come in me, come in my mouth . . .

Xxx Stella x

22.

The last fuck with the motherfucker

. . .

Marilyn's story

He told me how sexy I looked and how excited he was, so I took off my panties in the car. . .

Goddamn motherfucker. . .

Well, I do look good in the picture with the hot dress on. Thank you, sugar daddy, for buying me that dress. But still, goddamn you, motherfucker.

All right, so after losing the stupid contest, I texted motherfucker a hot picture of me in the hot dress and of course he came to the club to see me. My girlfriend said that it was her friend's birthday so I said let's take the birthday boy out to the strip club and I took the hot motherfucker with me.

We were at the strip club, drinking -- my alter ego comes out when I am drinking. I wanted to get on stage and he said okay I'll check if it's okay. So I went on stage and did a sexy dance around the pole, while sending over kisses to motherfucker.

When I came off the stage I asked motherfucker if he wanted a lap dance. He said fuck the lap dance, I want you, so I went home with him -- he was a sexy tall man and I just couldn't help myself.

We met outside and he opened the car door for me -- I had on the hot dress. He told me how sexy I looked and how excited he was and I took off my panties in the car. I took the panties off and I don't know who I gave them to. I don't even know when I took them off. I was wasted. I don't know what happened to them -- I probably won't get them back either. And they are not even my panties, I borrowed them from my girlfriend at the contest.

So we went home together to my house and I asked him to take off my dress. He kissed me on the neck and I went to the shower and got in. When I turned around, he was there, washing my ass and my coochie and my body and my neck. He started kissing me, then I got out of the shower, so he could take a shower. I was lying in bed drizzling lotion on myself when he got out of the shower, so he took the lotion away from me and gave me another foot massage.

He made me sit right behind him and he was pressing my coochie into his back while he was massaging my feet. I was horny and drunk and wow, he really turned me on. He turned me around and he went down on me. Then we were kissing and I turned him around so he was lying on his back and I was lying on top of him. I put my hands on his hands, so we were lying on top of each other and rubbing against each other, but I didn't let his dick come close to my coochie. That went on for a long, long time -- we had a long, long foreplay, kissing and rubbing against each other. Then he went down on me again -- it was hot, it was just hot, really hot. He put on the condom and we did it missionary style at first. Then he flipped me around and we did it doggie style. He likes to spread my cheeks, so he can choke his dick and get it in deeper.

Then he turned me around again and he had me put my hands on my ankles and spread them apart, so it looked like a V. He was stroking his dick inside me and was looking at me the whole time.

And he went down on me again, his tongue was licking my coochie and I was making so much noise, I don't know if the neighbors will be able to look me in the eyes. Oh god it was so good.

Well, we finally fell asleep and slept until probably 11 AM or so and then we started talking. He told me how sexy I was. He asked, do you know how to make the music play, because I have a saxophone tattooed on my thigh. I said, um mhummm, so we did 69 and he licked me until I came.

When I was coming, he was stroking deeper in my mouth. Then he came and I felt his warm come all over my mouth -- we were coming together. He said OMG, you're dangerous. And I said OMG, I won't hurt you.

So we both took showers and when I was in the shower, he made my bed.

We had been at the bar, and then we were in his truck, and then we were in the strip club, and then back in his truck, and then in the office when my girlfriend was there -- we were talking and we were kissing -- I was teasing him then -- and then we were back at my place. Oh yeah, it was so-o-o good -- we were fucking until the sun came up and for a long time afterwards too.

When I woke up in the morning, my pussy was sore and burning. I said oh, we must have been fucking a lot. He said, you don't remember? He was laughing and I said, are you going to refresh my memory?

Oh man, fuck, why did he have to do this shit. Now that I found out he's not divorced, I can't have him anymore. He's not even separated. . .

And I said motherfucker. And I have been saying it ever since. . .

Motherfucker. . .

I can't blame him, though. Man, if I were a dude I wouldn't have said no to me either. I was in a hot dress, I was wasted, I was horny, and I took my panties off.

Oh well, on to the next one. . .

23.

Come to the shower with me

. . .

Sara's story

"I'm going to take a shower and cover myself with soapy bubbles. My muff will look a shaving brush full of soapy pearls. I'm going to rub it all over you and get you soapy too. . ."

~ After the transatlantic flight

Sara:

I walked into the airline executive lounge room shower at the airport after I got off the long overnight flight back into the country . . . I had wanted to fuck you so much from the time I got off the plane, just after I landed, and even more when I was standing in line at immigration/reentry, waiting for my luggage. I wanted a shower so badly after flying for so long and just as much, I wanted to fuck you as I was standing in the shower room. The dark ceramic tiles on the wall were covered in beads of water from the shower, the mirrors were steamy and streaked with moisture, the towels were stacked thick and white on the slatted teak shelves on the wall, and I thought of you. I imagined you leaning back against the dark tiles, your golden haired balls, warm in my hand, your golden haired head bent over while your mouth sucked my nipples with your tongue rolling around them. Then I could feel your mouth on mine, our lips together and apart, together and apart, as your fingers twist and pinch my nipples, sending currents of heat down to my pussy. I can feel your skin against mine, so smooth together, against the dark, shiny, cold wet tiles . . .

~ A few days later

Sara: I'm off to the theatre to see an Aussie theatre troupe perform a Chekov classic --

And I'm leaving the house at the last minute, wearing sexy underwear that you can't see -- yet xx. . .

~ A few hours later

Sara:

I'm back home now.

I want you to watch me undress - here's the first few photos.

There are more photos, of course -- 21 of them in all.

You'll let me know when you want to see them, won't you? xx

Do you know I want to fuck you xx?

I do, I do mmmmmm . . .

Do you want me to lick you?

How do you want me to lick you?

Do you want to suck my nipples?

Shawn:

Wow xx

Now I have a hard on xx

Sara:

I'm going to take a shower and cover myself with soapy bubbles.

My muff will look like it is full of soapy pearls.

I'm going to rub myself all over you and get you soapy too, especially with my soapy bush, my soapy muff, full of bubbles, just like a shaving brush. . .

Back soon . . .

Sara: Sending picture . . .

> **Picture**: *Come to the shower with me (wet and naked, standing in shower door)*

Shawn

Very hard now x

Sara:

I'm going to soap you all over with my soapy muff ...

Then rinse it clean ...

Bury your face in my pussy and suck my clit...

Stick your tongue inside my cunt ...

Sara: Sending another picture . . .

Picture*: (Close up of soapy muff, lathered up)*

Shawn:

Very hard xx

Very horny xx

I want to fuck you xx xx xx

Sara:

Lick me xx ...

Rinse the soap off me and lick me xx

Shawn:

I would like to fuck you with your vibrator x

Sara:

Yes xx ...

I like xx ...

I'm going to the bedroom xx where the vibrators are ...

Tell me more...

I'm getting hot xx ...

I want you xx ...

I want your face in my pussy xx

Shawn:

I would lick you as the vibrator is deep inside you x

Sara:

Tell me more . . . Tell me more . . .

Shawn:

Then I want to suck your nipples while you play with the vibrator x

Sara:

Ooooh . . . mmmm. . .

Shawn:

Then I want to turn you around and smack your bum as I pinch your nipples and you play x

Sara:

Oh, I'm getting wet. . .

I can feel your hand print stinging on my bum xx

I love that xx

My nipples are getting hard . . .

Smack my bum harder... I'm so horny for you... I am very wet xx feel my cunt hot and wet xx

Shawn:

I want to watch you playing xxx

Sara:

Is this a one-way watch again?

You'll have to make me hotter than I am now xx

Make me really hot, so I can see you in my imagination xx

Can you talk this time?

I can't see what you type until afterwards -- still that was hot xx xx xx

I like what you said last time xx.

I got hot for you again later, when I read what you wrote xx

Shawn:

I can talk.

Send me an invite on Skype x

Sara:

Yes . . .

I'm setting up the laptop and lighting, doing wirey things. . .

Shawn:

I want to FUCK you xxx

Sara:

Ooooooh . . .

I want to fuck you too, oh do I want to fuck you xx. . .

Okay, magic man, help me out.

Get on Skype

I want to fuck you xx.

Oooo, I can see you xx.

Where are you?

At the beach?

Shawn:

Near the beach.

Outside in the sun, sitting by my pool.

Sara:

Oh wow,

I can see all of you now, there you are. . .

Pull out your cock for me. . .

You are so gorgeous, hot sexy man.

I love looking at your great hard dick.

If you were here, I would have my lips wrapped around your dick and it would be deep inside my mouth.

Here, taste my pussy . . .

Lick it off my fingers, sexy man . . .

Suck my pussy juice off fingers and taste me as you watch me play and you stroke . . .

Now watch me come, with my vibrator in my cunt and my fingers pinching my nipples . . .

Spurt your come so I can see it too. . .

Oh, oh, oh, I can see you explode, I see your come. . .

Now, rub your fingers in your come -- hold them up to my mouth and let me lick them . . .

24.

Monday night is massage night

. . .

Roxy's story

I said don't fall in love and he said what?
I said you can be my boy toy . . .

I met this guy once when we were out partying and I was totally attracted to him. He was BUILT. He had muscles and these long dreads. . . I thought, ooooh you can get in it, honey -- my coochie, you can get right in there.

I could tell he was interested in me, but I did not want to get into a another relationship so soon after the last one -- and that's another story right there, but I'll tell you about that one later. . . You know, after my first date with him, I said don't fall in love and he said what? And I said, don't fall in love, just be my boy toy.

That night we started dancing. We were touching and grinding on each other, then went to tongue kissing -- we both got horny when my tongue found his tongue piercing. My girlfriend was talking to his friend and I thought damn, because my friend was going to sleep at my house that night, so there was no way of me getting anything more from him, but I really wanted him.

Luckily, my friend asked me, what are we going to do? I don't know, I said, because we both wanted to have sex with those guys. I ended up giving her the keys to my place and I went with the guy with the tongue stud.

He was already touching me in the car -- he was driving this little red speedy sports car playing loud music, heavy with bass that I thought was so ghetto, I wasn't sure if he was going to be romantic.

We drove to his place and parked. He had a townhouse on three levels -- open plan architecture, so you could look into the living room. He handed me a towel and turned on the shower for me. I had a nice, long hot shower and I thought ooooh this is going to be good -- you know, I'm getting excited just remembering this.

When I finished my shower, I found that he had lit candles and had slow music playing. He lay me down on the bed, kissed me, and turned me around on my tummy, and started massaging my back with baby oil. He was very slow and sensual . . . He was breathing in rhythm with the massage strokes, so it was almost like a tantric massage. Then he turned me around and went down on me and I tell you, honey -- that piercing felt really good.

He told me he wanted to please me, he said that's all he wanted to do. He kissed me again and massaged my breasts with the baby oil. Then he touched my legs as he went down on me -- it was a combination of the massage, the kisses, and his licking that made me really hot. He could tell I was about to come, so he stopped and got the condom. I thought, like yeah, let's get it . . . then he went down on me again and got me to where I was almost coming before he entered me. . . he was good, I mean, oh god, he was really, really good. He was stroking and holding my head while he was kissing me and telling me how good I felt, which turned me on even more. He was so gentle -- we just fucked all night, until the morning when we fell asleep

In the morning, we woke up and I knew I couldn't kiss him, because I had morning breath, but he turned toward me and started kissing me -- I thought, OMG he's a freak. He had pleased me all night, so now I wanted to please him.

He had these nipple piercings, so I started kissing his piercings -- all around them. I kissed his stomach and I knew that he had been working out, because he had this nice six pack. I went down and found he had shaved his pubs -- I liked that. His dick was nice and smooth -- I really liked sucking it. I thought now it's my turn to make you crazy, so I did the same as he did -- I got him to where he was almost ready to come, then I grabbed the condom, put it on him, and eased his dick into my coochie, as I sat on him. I got him to where I almost made him explode, then I stopped and just kissed him, really deep, romantic kisses -- I knew he liked kissing like this while fucking. Then I started riding him again . . . He told me he didn't want to come yet, so he flipped me around and started licking me -- that's when we came together.

We started talking and I found out he was a personal trainer, so I thought what a jackpot. That's when I asked him if he was okay with being my boy toy and he said that was just fine with him.

We looked at our schedules and found out that we only had time to see each other on Monday nights. I got up to leave and said see you next Monday then.

So that was how we met. . .

I was really looking forward to the next Monday, so much that I almost called him every day, I really wanted to see him again so much, but I thought it would be better just to wait -- this way, we would both be really horny when we saw each other.

Monday finally came. He called me and asked me what I wanted to have for dinner. I asked him what he liked. We found out that we loved sushi. He also asked me what I liked to drink and I told him he could choose something himself.

I spent the afternoon getting ready for our date -- and you know how ready I got -- waxing, shaving, rubbing lotion all over my body, so my skin would be soft -- I felt like a teenager on the first date.

When I arrived at his house, he was waiting for me. He had sushi and wine ready for dinner, and had gotten a romantic comedy to watch. I thought, I could get used to this, lying back with him on his comfy couch, with no drama and no cell phones ringing . . .

At the end of the movie, we started making out on the couch and taking each others clothes off. We were a little tipsy already, so we just couldn't make it upstairs to the bedroom. We ended up fucking right there, bending over on the couch, then rolling around all over the living room.

When we finished, I thought that I should leave -- you know, like no sleep over -- but he took my hand and led me to the bedroom. We lay down and he held me and hugged me and kissed me until we fell asleep together, curled up like spoons. In the morning, he woke up early because he had to leave for work at 5 AM. I said, oh man I am not a morning person at all, so he gave me his house key, told me to lock the door when I left, and said he'd see me next Monday. Ohhh, how I really looked forward to each Monday night -- I still have his key, even though it ended between us long ago.

Now, you know how I feel about all these other guys, but this guy . . . Oh, man, he was just amazing.

Stella Regina Maris

Stella has been composing prose and verse as long as she can remember.

When she is not eavesdropping on intimate conversations in coffee houses, Stella spends most of her time in an airplane -- or waiting to get on one.

www.ingramcontent.com/pod-product-compliance
Lightning Source LLC
Chambersburg PA
CBHW030024180626
46810CB00001B/202